Natalie bit back a scream as the door pressed solidly, inch by inch, against the pile of furniture. A hand snaked into the room, connecting with the top of a chair and shoving it off the pile.

Then a loud shout came from down the hall and the gloved hand retreated.

She stood rooted to her spot, her imagination running wild. What if Luke needed help? What if an accomplice was heading toward the room right now?

She jumped back when a rap sounded at the door.

"It's me."

Luke!

He peered into the gap between the door and the wall, eyeing the furniture.

"I'll come through my room," he said, and disappeared from view. Mere seconds passed before he unlocked his side and rushed into her room.

"Are you okay?" He stepped close to her, his gaze assessing.

She nodded, because she couldn't find her voice.

"I'm sorry. I thought it was a trap. I shouldn't have left you here. We need to get moving." Luke was already packing his belongings into his backpack. "We'll find somewhere else to stay tonight. It's not safe here."

Sara K. Parker has been a writer ever since she was gifted a 4x6 pin-striped journal for her tenth birthday. Her writing hobby has since grown into her dream career—writing for Love Inspired, freelancing for magazines and teaching English at a community college. She and her husband live in northwest Houston with their four children, two (soon to be three!) mischievous dogs and an extremely vocal senior cat.

Books by Sara K. Parker

Love Inspired Suspense

Undercurrent
Dying to Remember
Shattered Trust

SHATTERED TRUST

SARA K. PARKER

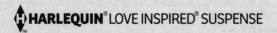
HARLEQUIN® LOVE INSPIRED® SUSPENSE

LOVE INSPIRED BOOKS

Recycling programs
for this product may
not exist in your area.

ISBN-13: 978-1-335-23200-7

Shattered Trust

www.Harlequin.com

Printed in U.S.A.

When thou passest through the waters, I will be with thee; and through the rivers, they shall not overflow thee: when thou walkest through the fire, thou shalt not be burned; neither shall the flame kindle upon thee.
–Isaiah 43:2

To my siblings: Mary Ellen, Shirlee, Beth and Jonathan.
For showing up on my doorstep when I needed you most.
I love you.

ONE

It wasn't the first time anyone had been stood up at the altar, but it would be the only time Natalie Harper was.

She was perfectly capable of being happy alone, and she would be.

Inhaling the briny sea air, she stared hard into the darkening sunset along the horizon, willing herself not to give in to the flood of humiliation that kept pressing in on her. Plenty of women had walked this same path before her. Thousands of dollars and months of planning wasted on a romantic waterside ceremony and festive reception—and no groom in attendance. But she was probably one of only a renegade few who dared to flee the aftermath and embark on a solo honeymoon. It felt just a little bit selfish now that she was lying on a pristine beach, the sky painted vibrant colors as the sun set along the Riviera Maya.

Night was falling quickly, and up and down the beach, most people had already deserted their loungers and cabanas and headed back to their hotels. Natalie knew she should, too. She twisted around to scan her surroundings, to assure herself she was truly alone. The nearby loungers sat empty, dilapidated sand castles the only sign that anyone had been there at all. The scene should have been peaceful, but the darkness beyond made her uneasy.

Staring hard into the shadows, Natalie saw no signs of movement, nothing to account for the goose bumps rising on her arms.

Turning back to the fading sun, she reasoned with herself that her uneasiness was a product of fear, not proof of a lurker in the shadows. She'd fought that anxiety for close to twenty years now, and she knew it well. She forced herself to relax again and try to enjoy the solace, even if she didn't particularly enjoy solitude or beach vacations.

Her fiancé had chosen the location, and Natalie had gone along with the plan. If she'd had her way, they would have rented a cabin somewhere along the Shenandoah River, hiked quiet wooded paths and just enjoyed being together.

She didn't often get her way, though, and reserved her battles for the issues that truly mattered—right versus wrong, life versus death, milk chocolate versus dark.

In the end, a resort in Mexico versus a cabin in Virginia wasn't an argument worth having, so she'd let it go.

And then… Kyle Paxton had let *her* go.

She stopped her thoughts in their tracks. She had seven more days to process all that had happened and decide how to move on. Tonight, she didn't want to think.

She didn't want to think about her string of failed relationships or Kyle's poorly timed cold feet. She didn't want to think about facing her family's well-meaning sympathy, returning the mountain of wedding gifts waiting for her at home or unpacking her lonely boxed-up apartment. Taking a sip of her now-lukewarm strawberry lemonade, her gaze caught on the gaudy engagement ring on her finger.

She didn't want to think about the ugly ring, either—a knock-off of the $1.4 million original worn by her friend and rising actress, Julianna Montgomery, last year at the

Golden Globes. Julianna hadn't won best actress, but her red carpet look had captured the world's attention—from her body-skimming midnight blue gown to her wildly expensive jewelry, including the ring. Now Natalie stared down at the replica, its one-carat marquise diamond flanked by an army of teardrop sapphires jutting around the center like the sun's rays, and wondered why she hadn't handed it straight back to her fiancé. She'd hated it, but hadn't had the heart to tell him, or the willingness to think about what his choice of rings meant.

Natalie liked quiet, elegant things, timeless styles, understated beauty. The pretentious ring only symbolized how little her fiancé truly knew her…and how much time and energy Natalie had poured into a relationship with someone who didn't care enough about her to learn her tastes.

She glared down at the ring, the setting sun glowing in the depth of its stones. Maybe the first step to moving forward with new dreams was letting go of the old ones—the turnkey house in the heart of Baltimore, the pretty yard and the porch with flower baskets hanging from its eaves. The kids, the dog, the minivan. Were those even her own dreams in the first place? They had all been wrapped up in the copycat ring and Kyle's empty promises, both of which had fallen far short of her expectations.

Twisting the too-tight band, she struggled to shimmy it over her knuckle. It had been a snug fit from the start, but the beach heat had caused her fingers to swell slightly. She'd considered dropping the ring off to be resized at her friend's jewelry shop, but Hannah was already struggling to keep up with orders while her dad fought stage four glioblastoma. Natalie didn't want to add to the burden, but she didn't want to hurt Hannah's feelings by bringing the ring somewhere else. It wasn't really a problem, anyway, except for whenever she tried to take it off. She finally released her finger from its grip and held the ring between her thumb and forefinger, her attention straying to the endless black water beyond. It seemed the perfect place to toss it, the cloud-dimmed moon a silent witness to her rejection of all the ring had come to symbolize.

But Natalie's practicality won, as it usually did, and instead she stuffed the ring into her shorts pocket. Maybe she could sell it and pay her dad back some of the money he'd wasted on the wedding that hadn't happened.

A whisper of movement sounded behind her and she sat up in her chair, her feet settling into the still-warm sand. Large umbrellas shadowed clusters of vacated lounge chairs. Still empty. Every one of them. But darkness had fallen and she couldn't see far beyond her solitary spot. A shifting shadow sent her pulse leaping, but she blinked and it was gone. Had she imagined it? It didn't matter. Natalie had stayed too long.

She shoved her feet back into sand-filled flip-flops and tucked her book and sunscreen into her bag. All the while, she scanned the lonely beach, straining to hear anything unusual above the splash of the waves along the shore behind her.

Nothing, but she felt hunted, and that scared her.

Hurriedly, she bent to retrieve her towel, but as she straightened, a dark form emerged from behind a pair of loungers just yards away. Her breath caught in her throat and for one second, she froze, the towel dropping from her hand. And then the man lunged toward her, a knife glinting in his hand. Natalie screamed, swiveling away and taking off across the beach, all energy focused on the outline of the hotel against the moonlit sky.

Don't look back, don't look back! But she couldn't help it. She looked back.

And then she wished she hadn't. Because he was too close and too fast. And the hotel was too far away. Even as she pushed for more speed, sand flying up behind her on the beach, even as she focused every bit of energy on the hotel lights far ahead, his harsh breathing bore down on her, his footsteps closing in. In a panic, she surged forward, her leg muscles screaming from the effort, but her shorter frame was no match for his long legs.

A hand snatched at the back of her shirt and she screamed again, tearing away and dodging his grasp. But her foot hit an uneven mound of sand, and she went flying, her palms barely breaking her fall as her attacker's arms snaked around her middle and yanked her backward. She screamed in desperation, hoping someone would hear and come to her rescue, but the sharp point of a knife pressed into the side of her throat, and she stilled.

The rough edge of his bandanna rubbed the side of Natalie's face, and repulsion slid up her throat as his mouth pressed close to her ear. "Shut up," he commanded, his stale breath hot at her neck.

He was going to kill her. Natalie knew that as surely as she knew that screaming and kicking would only hasten her death. One wrong move and the blade would puncture her throat, and she'd be left to bleed out as the tide came up and washed her body away.

Luke Everett was just about to give up his search and try again back at the hotel when he heard the screams. Now he sprinted across the empty beach toward the voice he'd heard, hoping the screams hadn't come from the woman he'd been searching for. His hope was short-lived as he came upon the scene—Natalie Harper restrained by a stranger in black, a knife to her throat.

Luke's blood ran cold.

Natalie had gone still, her attacker behind her, one arm hooked around her waist, the other across her chest with a menacing grip on the knife. Her captor met Luke's eyes, his face hidden by shadows and a dark bandanna. A local, Luke thought. Young-ish. Several inches taller than Natalie. He filed the information away as the man dragged Natalie back a few steps.

Her panicked eyes locked on him, pleading silently for help.

"Get out of here!" the man snapped, pressing the blade deeper against Natalie's pale flesh. No accent. Maybe not a local after all.

Luke took a step closer. "Let her go."

"I said, *leave*!" the man bit out. "This isn't your business."

"I think it is," Luke responded, shifting to the right, trying to get in position to disarm the guy. But the man's eyes were shrewd, and they all knew he had the upper hand.

One week of 24/7 work covertly guarding the adult daughter of a federal judge had seemed like the perfect assignment—low threat and all expenses paid in a prime resort on the beach. There'd been no indication that Natalie was in any kind of danger, that there would be any threat against her. Her father had simply wanted to be sure she was okay.

She wasn't.

Not by a long shot.

The attacker tracked Luke's every move, eyes gleaming above the bandanna. Then his grip on Natalie loosened, the knife moving away from her neck as he jabbed it toward Luke.

"Back off," he growled. "Or someone's gonna get hurt."

He jabbed the knife again, and Natalie shifted, meeting Luke's eyes.

She was going to try to break free, Luke was sure of it.

"Don't—" he started to say, but she was already moving, dropping all of her weight against the arm that held her. Her assailant stumbled, and she twisted, darting to the side as the knife arced through the air. Luke sprang forward, shoving the guy with both hands, the blade barely missing his face. He thought it might have glanced off Natalie's shoulder, but he couldn't be sure. He was too focused on the fight, on getting the advantage and keeping the attacker from doing any more damage.

Grabbing the guy's wrist, he twisted it up behind his back until the knife dropped to the ground. He kicked it away, sand covering the gleaming blade.

"Run!" Luke yelled to Natalie, wrestling the attacker down into too-soft sand that made a locked grip nearly impossible.

Natalie ran, all right. Straight to her beach chair and her overloaded bag.

For about three seconds, Luke thought she was going for the bag because she didn't want to leave her valuables behind. Then she was back, swinging the bag toward the man's head.

It hit the man's shoulder, glancing off his head with a muffled thud.

"Natalie, run!" Luke repeated.

Too late. The assailant snagged her ankle with his free hand, yanking hard enough to unbalance her. She fell sideways, knocking into Luke with enough force to send them both falling. He grabbed her automatically, cushioning her fall as they both rolled into the sand.

Before Luke could right himself, the attacker was sprinting away, Natalie's bag under his arm.

"Hey!" she yelled, and darted forward to run after him.

Luke caught her arm. "Let him go."

"He took my bag."

"Better than taking your life." He pulled out his phone and shone the flashlight on a dark stain on the shoulder of her light blue T-shirt.

Natalie frowned, pulling the fabric aside and eyeing a three-inch cut on her shoulder.

"Here." Luke bent down and snapped up her towel, handing it to her. "Press this to your shoulder."

He shrugged out of his light jacket and used it to pick up the discarded knife, depositing the weapon into a pocket of his tactical pants. He was anxious to get back to the hotel, to get a better look at the cut. That had been close. If he'd arrived even a few minutes later… He wouldn't let himself think about that. He'd gotten there on time, and Natalie was safe. No thanks to the gun Luke had been forced to leave at home because of international travel restrictions.

To think he'd barely blinked when his boss, Roman DeHart, had informed him he'd have to travel unarmed. He'd need to give Roman a call about the incident, and he wasn't looking forward to that. Not that Roman would give him flak. The two had been longtime friends before Luke had started working at Shield Protection Services. But Roman wouldn't relish having to break the news to Judge Harper that his daughter had ended up in the hospital with a knife wound on her first night in Mexico.

A protective arm at Natalie's back, Luke quickly led the way up the beach and onto the sandy path back to the Riu de Sueños Hotel. Coconut palms and sea-grape trees lined the path, offering plenty of cover for anyone who might want to lie in wait for unsuspecting tourists.

Was that what the assailant had been? An opportunist? Someone who'd seen an easy mark and acted?

Luke studied the shadows, looking for signs that they weren't alone, but he saw no one. The ocean's rush mingled with a whisper of wind through the treetops and the quiet murmur of conversation from hotel guests who stood on balconies and patios.

A normal evening along the Riviera.

Except that Natalie was hurt, her attacker on the loose, her belongings stolen.

Lively music echoed from the hotel, the sound of voices beckoning the pair to safety. He picked up the pace, and Natalie had no trouble keeping up.

As soon as the glass doors slid open and Natalie and Luke stepped inside, he discreetly led her to the front desk and asked for hotel security.

The desk attendant glanced at the pair with curiosity, but with Natalie's wound covered, her injury wasn't apparent.

"One moment, sir," the woman said, and picked up her radio to contact security.

Several long minutes later, a lone security officer walked casually toward them, his polished dress shoes knocking along the tile floor.

"I am Officer Canto. How may I help you?" he asked, his English as perfect as his tailored navy uniform. A young guy, new to security, Luke judged.

"This woman was attacked at knifepoint on the beach," Luke responded. "She's injured. Her attacker dropped the weapon and ran off with her purse."

The security officer's attention shifted to Natalie, his bland expression unchanged. "You are injured?" he asked, as if requiring proof.

Natalie lifted the towel from her shoulder, and Officer Canto's eyes widened at the bloodstained fabric. "Please, follow me," he said, his voice urgent now. He walked at a clipped pace, speaking rapid-fire Spanish into his radio as they followed.

Luke wasn't impressed. If the mere sight of a little blood was all it took to send the guy into panic mode, Luke didn't plan to entrust their safety to him or his team. But they would have to follow protocol and file a report, at least, so he didn't see any other option but to follow him as the officer ushered them down the hall behind the lobby. He finally opened a door into a small office with a single desk and three padded folding chairs. No windows.

"Please, sit. I will get a fresh towel." The officer left the room, shutting the door behind him. Natalie sat, but Luke remained standing, fighting the urge to open the door to the hallway. Some people felt safer in enclosed spaces. Luke felt trapped.

If a first-grade teacher hadn't cared enough to push for answers, Luke might have died in the closet his mother's boyfriend had locked him in years ago. Four days alone in the dark with no food and barely any water? That did a number on a person. He eyed the door. He wasn't a scrawny seven-year-old anymore. He pushed the unwanted memory away and focused on Natalie.

"Let me take a look at that," Luke said, gently taking the towel from her and pushing the bloodstained T-shirt away from her shoulder.

She winced, her face devoid of color, amber eyes flashing pain.

"It's pretty deep. Better keep pressure on it," he said, setting the towel back in place. "I'm no doctor, but it looks like you'll need some stitches."

"I should have stayed home," she muttered.

"You couldn't have known you'd be attacked on the beach," Luke pointed out, but could see his words didn't have much effect, her eyes sad. A light spattering of freckles made her look younger than her twenty-nine years. Her near-white blond hair was short and wavy, a delicate pearl hair pin askew over one ear. He'd been informed about her fiancé standing her up at the altar. She'd decided to go on her honeymoon anyway, and by all rights, she should have been able to enjoy a few quiet evenings on a beach after something like that.

Natalie was eyeing him curiously. "Thank you for coming to my rescue... It's a good thing you were there. I'm Natalie Harper, by the way... But then, you knew that already."

"Luke Everett," he introduced himself, knowing that after calling out her name on the beach earlier, he couldn't exactly keep his identity from her. "I'm with Shield. Your dad hired me to watch out for you on this trip."

"Of course he did." She didn't look surprised. She looked resigned.

"You don't look happy about it."

She shrugged, flashing a half-hearted smile. "My father is overprotective. It gets a little old. Tonight, though, I'm thankful for it."

Her dad's borderline obsession with his family's security was well respected within Shield. Almost twenty years ago, the Harpers had lost their only son in a tragic abduction that had ended in the little boy's murder. Natalie and her twin sister had been eight or nine at the time. Luke could see how growing up under the watchful eye of an always-present security team could feel suffocating and intrusive.

The office door opened and the officer reentered, handing a fresh towel to Natalie. Then he skirted the small desk and typed on the computer keyboard as Natalie folded the stained towel into her lap and applied the new one to the wound.

"First, what is your name, miss?" the officer asked.

"Natalie Harper," she stated. "Room 112."

Officer Canto used only his two index fingers to type, his data entry excruciatingly slow. Luke groaned inwardly, but then Natalie glanced his way, a comical eyebrow raised in camaraderie, and he almost laughed. Forcing himself to relax, he leaned against the wall, settling in for what looked like would be a lengthy interview.

Luke listened and watched as Natalie recounted the details of the attack with precision and a surprising calm. The only visible sign of stress he'd caught was the slight tremor in her hand when she pushed her hair behind her ear.

But then, Natalie had grown up in the public eye. She was also a PR exec at a prestigious firm in downtown Baltimore, definitely not a person who would easily collapse under pressure.

"Can you describe the assailant?" the officer asked.

"He was taller than me by several inches," she answered. "Not quite six feet. Medium build, but muscular. Wearing all black. Gloves. A bandanna. I couldn't really see his face."

"Tattoos? Scars? Hair color?" the officer prompted.

"His hair was dark. Brown or black. Straight, short. I didn't see any tattoos or scars." She looked at Luke. "Did you?"

He shook his head, pushing off from the wall and grabbing a tissue from a box on the desk. "No. But this is his knife." Using the tissue, he retrieved the knife from his pocket and set it on the desk.

The officer's eyes narrowed in on Luke. "Are you two traveling together?"

"I'm part of her private security team." No need for

anyone to know the rest of the team was back in the States.

"Most people do not bring private security to our resort."

"Considering what happened tonight," Luke said, "perhaps they should."

The officer scowled, but didn't respond. Instead, he slowly clicked a few more keys on his keyboard and then turned his attention back to them. "I am very sorry for your experience," he said—with questionable sincerity. "We will investigate the matter." He pulled open a drawer and handed Luke his business card before crossing the tight room and opening the door for them.

Natalie stood to leave, but Luke didn't budge. No way would he let the matter stand like this, trusting the resort's security team to properly investigate the assault. "I'd like to speak with local police right away," he said. "Would you call an officer to the hotel?"

"I have called already. We will ring your room when an officer arrives." He motioned to the door again, dismissing them.

"Ms. Harper will need a new room," Luke pointed out, still not making a move to leave. The mugger would have access to her key card in her purse, so new security measures would need to be put in place. "And we'll need transportation to a nearby clinic where she can have her injury taken care of."

The officer hesitated for the briefest of moments before nodding. "I will arrange for transportation. Let us go speak with the front desk about the room."

Despite the less than impressive security response at the hotel, the staff at the front desk were efficient and accommodating. Within minutes, Natalie and Luke were all set, new key cards in hand for side-by-side rooms on the seventh floor.

Luke wished he'd arrived just a little sooner that evening, but it'd been impossible to get an earlier flight. At least he'd gotten to the beach in time to intervene, or things could have been a whole lot worse.

Maybe it had been a crime of opportunity. *Maybe*. But Luke wasn't going to take any chances. The woman wouldn't leave his sight for the next seven days, except to use the bathroom and sleep. If he was honest with himself, he'd be a lot more comfortable with backup right about now. He felt a little out of his element since he'd been slowly cutting back his hours at Shield over the past several months in favor of devoting more time to the community center he was trying to get off the ground.

The project had been a dream for years, but after a gunshot wound on assignment last year, he'd decided it was time to make the dream a reality. Renovations were well underway on the building he had leased, and grant money had been flowing in. But when Roman had called to offer him the contract, Luke hadn't hesitated to accept. Roman had been convincing enough—mentioning how short-staffed Shield was at the moment, as well as how handy Luke's minor in Spanish would be. But when Luke heard the payout, he was sold. His sister, Triss, was heading into her last year of college, and he had the idea to use the paycheck to surprise her by covering her next tuition bill.

But first, the task at hand. They'd need to gather their belongings and transport them up to the new rooms. As they approached Natalie's old room, Luke's hand came to her elbow, keeping her close.

"Allow me," he said, reaching over to take the key card from her.

"I can manage," she responded, swiping the card in front of the lock mechanism.

Luke's hand covered hers on the handle. "Someone has your old key. I'm not taking any chances."

After all, Natalie had been entrusted to his care. Sure, guarding her was a job, and he was getting paid to do it, but he took the work as seriously as he'd taken raising his younger siblings after he'd won custody. His commitment. His responsibility.

"Fair point," she said, her hand sliding out from under his palm. She didn't stand back, though. Instead, she drew a little closer, and he caught a whiff of salty air and sunscreen mixed with a citrusy scent that could have been shampoo or perfume.

Her nearness triggered an unexpected attraction, Luke's pulse surging double-time. He steadfastly ignored it. He'd learned his lesson two years ago, and he'd remember it. The workplace was no place for romance. Especially the private security workplace, where emotions often ran high and created a false sense of connection.

He pushed the thoughts aside and opened the door, flicking on the light as he stepped into the room.

A suitcase lay on the floor, clothes dumped beside it. The mattress had been tossed from the bed, sheets and pillows thrown into a pile. Balmy air billowed in from the open sliding glass door, dark shadows undulating on the balcony behind it.

An escape route for the intruder? Or a hiding place?

He wasn't going to investigate. Not with Natalie stepping into the room behind him.

"What—" she started, but he grabbed her arm, tugging her back over the threshold and into the hall. The room was silent and still—no sign of an intruder lying in wait. He eyed the closed closet door and the one that opened into the bathroom, then fixed his attention back on the balcony. The perp had entered that way. Or he'd entered through the door and left that way. *If* he'd left. Luke reached into the room and flicked off the light, watching the shadows play on the balcony curtains.

"Do you—"

"Shhhhh," he whispered in Natalie's ear.

She stilled, and he knew she was watching the curtains, knew she was seeing what he did—a subtle shift in the shadows that seemed out of sync with the fluttering fabric.

A person? Or just the exterior lights playing tricks on his eyes? There. Gone. There again. He thought he heard a soft thud, a quiet rustle of fabric. Then the wind shifted, the curtains fell back into place and the balcony went still and silent once again.

TWO

It was closing in on midnight as Natalie finished sorting through her belongings. The police had taken photos and dusted for prints, and had been hovering with notepads ever since.

Luke didn't hover.

He helped, lifting the heavier items, asking questions about what she'd brought and what she still had. So far, it appeared the thief had stolen her passport, her cell phone, the two-hundred dollars she had stored in the room's safe and her small stash of jewelry. Everything else seemed to be accounted for, including her laptop, along with the barely-used bottle of Gucci perfume Kyle had given her for her birthday.

Natalie gave the room a final once-over. "I think that's all."

"Can you describe the missing jewelry?" Officer Perez asked. He'd been the first police officer on the scene, and his demeanor was empathetic and professional. His suit was a crisp clean tan, a contrast to the weathered lines on his face and his disheveled graying hair.

"Diamond studs." Her dad had given them to her when she turned sixteen. "A few pieces of costume jewelry that aren't worth much. A single strand pearl necklace." Her great-grandmother's. Aside from the earrings, it was the only thing she was really going to miss.

Natalie's bottom lip trembled and she turned away, busying herself with collecting a few more articles of clothing from the floor.

"And the value of the items?"

"The earrings, under five-hundred dollars. We had the necklace appraised a few years ago for twelve hundred."

"Everything else is accounted for?"

She remembered tucking a few pieces of jewelry into her makeup bag, and she walked into the bathroom to see if the thief had gotten to them, too.

"Yes," she said, pulling out two silver-chained necklaces and a handful of beaded bracelets. Not valuable. "That's everything."

"We will need you both to come to the station for fingerprints in the morning."

"How about we just drop by after we go to the hospital?" Luke suggested, looking to Natalie for agreement. "The sooner we get this over with, the sooner we can deal with the missing passport and get you out of here."

"Right." Her passport. She'd need it to get home—and it went without saying that home was where she needed to be.

She grabbed a pair of sandals and snagged the first outfit she saw. "I need to change. Then we can go."

The four officers in the room filed out the door and into the hallway. "We will wait outside," Officer Perez said.

Luke didn't follow.

Natalie waited.

He still didn't leave.

"You can wait with them," she nudged.

"No. I can't."

"But—"

"Natalie, I'm not leaving you in the room alone. There's no exterior entrance to the bathroom. You can change there."

That was it. Just a pronouncement, which in normal circumstances would have made her bristle. But tonight the words were a comfort, a source of security. Since getting on the airplane this morning, Natalie had never felt so alone in her life. But Luke wasn't about to leave her alone for a minute.

She walked into the bathroom and shut the door, her hands shaking as she changed out of her beach clothes, her shoulder throbbing under the bandages the hotel staff had rounded up. Sand scattered from her clothes onto the cool tile floor, and she changed quickly into a clean pair of jeans and a white tank top, splashed water on her face and then patted her skin dry with a towel. Her hair was a wreck, but there wasn't much she could do about the now-limp curls her hairdresser had carefully styled early that morning. She plucked the pearl hair pin out of her hair and ran her fingers through the tangles, noticing the deep pink along her nose and cheeks. Reapplying sunscreen had been the furthest thing from her mind earlier. She'd just been relieved to have snagged a flight out early that afternoon, and happy to have some time alone. Otherwise, she would have been stuck in a hotel room back in Maryland until her scheduled Sunday-morning flight, with no excuse not to answer her phone or open her door to concerned friends and family.

Luke knocked. "You okay?"

"Yes, I'll be right there." Leaving her hair for later, she scooped up her discarded clothing from the floor, reaching for the door. But the distinct clink of metal on tile stopped her, and she glanced at the ground to see her engagement ring rolling to a stop near the shower. She bent down to retrieve it, light flashing off the stones, the gaudiness of it reminding her of the lavish wedding Kyle had insisted they plan. The bigger, the better. That's what he'd said, and she'd agreed because it had seemed easier than arguing.

She glanced at the trash can, but knew she couldn't just discard the band. She might not like it, but throwing it away would be a selfish waste.

She grabbed a silver necklace chain from her makeup bag, replacing its heart pendant with the ugly ring before clasping the necklace behind her neck—for safekeeping rather than sentiment. Letting the heavy weight of the ring drop beneath her shirt, she opened the door and found Luke standing right at the threshold. He stepped back to let her pass, his dark brown eyes searching hers.

"Ready to go?"

Something about the way he looked at her, genuine concern in his gaze, made Natalie look away. "Almost," she said, sidling past him and shoving her beach clothes and toiletry bag into her suitcase.

It was a lie. She wasn't ready. She could handle the sympathetic looks from her family and friends. She could handle returning all the gifts and packing away her gown. But seeing Kyle again?

Her face burned at the thought as she and Luke grabbed her strewn belongings and packed them away. She never would have thought Kyle could be so heartless. So selfish. How dare he go through the motions of the elaborate rehearsal dinner, enjoy a night on the town with his buddies and then send her a text to cancel the wedding?

She zipped the suitcase and then her backpack carry-on.

"Is that everything?" Luke asked, slinging the carry-on over his shoulder and grabbing the suitcase by the handle.

She nodded.

"We'll ask at the front desk to have your luggage transferred to the new room." He reached with his free hand and opened the door for her.

Officer Perez stood just outside the door, the others having already dispersed. He nodded in greeting and led them down the hall toward the hotel lobby. The corridor was silent, the only sounds the tap of their shoes and the rolling of the suitcase along the tile. Natalie shivered, fear crawling up her neck as the entryway came into view. Her attacker was out there somewhere. Had he stuck around? Was he following them? Watching?

Luke paused at the reception desk to hand over the luggage, and Natalie turned back, peering down the hall.

"He'd be a fool to hang around," Luke said, drawing close. "But if he does, he won't get anywhere near you."

His hand came to her back, surprising her with its warmth and familiarity as he guided her toward the glass doors that led to the parking lot. He smelled like sunshine and salt water and something indefinably masculine. For a fraction of a second, she was tempted to slide her arm around his back and lean into his side.

Obviously, exhaustion was making her mind do funny things. As the hotel doors slid open in front of them, she folded her arms at her middle and away from Luke and the unwanted feelings threatening to surface.

Darkness edged the parking lot. A gentle wind rippled over her shoulders, leaving a chill in its wake, despite the warmth of the evening. She shivered, and Luke draped his jacket over her shoulders, careful of the wound.

"Thank you," she murmured.

Luke opened the rear-passenger door, waiting for her

to slide into the back seat before he did the same. She should have been disappointed to leave as the cruiser pulled away from the hotel, but she wanted to get as far away as possible, as quickly as possible.

"How hard do you think it'll be to get a new passport?" she asked Luke.

"Not sure. We'll need to go to the consulate's office. It's closed on Sundays."

Natalie bit back her disappointment and the car fell silent as the ocean view disappeared and the car sped along a narrow tree-lined road toward the hospital. Darkness shrouded the area, stars disappearing behind gathering clouds. A storm was coming. Even so, the clouds weren't yet thick enough to mask the glimmer of moonlight along the treetops ahead. And with the car windows cracked to the sea-scented breeze, the quiet beauty of the scene soothed some of Natalie's nerves. *God is here, even on roads filled with shadows and pathways shrouded in darkness.* That's what the world seemed to whisper, what the distant crash of the ocean surf seemed to say.

But for years, Natalie had struggled to believe it was true.

Had God been there on that beach with her tonight? Without a doubt. But what about everything else? The lost relationship she'd thought was a sure thing, her uncertain plans for the future? What about her brother's murder? Her mother's slow decline into a depression that would eventually take her life? Where was God in those dark hours? Those were questions with no easy answers, questions that made her faith seem hollow, her prayers feel empty. She blinked back the sudden sting of tears, pushed the questions away like she always did and took a steadying breath. But as the streetlights appeared farther and farther apart and the ocean disappeared from view, a suffocating sense of fear took hold. Somewhere, her attacker was out there. Would she make it home before he found her again?

"You have a security system back at your place?"

Luke's question yanked her out of her thoughts, and she glanced his way. "I do. But I never use it. Do you really think trouble will follow me there?"

"Doesn't seem likely," Luke said, but he didn't look convinced. "It's always safest to plan for the worst."

Natalie preferred to plan for the best, but she had to admit that Luke's strategy was wiser. She'd been impressed with Shield Protection Services since her father started contracting with them a few years ago, but she'd never personally worked with anyone from the company. He'd used another company for years before he'd realized that it was time to downsize his security measures. Natalie and her sister, Kristin, had been out of the house for quite some time, and he'd started to realize that he'd gone a little overboard while they were growing up.

Natalie couldn't blame him. She imagined she may have been just like him if Liam had been her son and she'd had two little girls to protect as a single parent. But growing up with a parent who was obsessed with safety had set her up for all kinds of fears that she continued to battle as an adult. After tonight, she couldn't help but consider that her father's fears may not have been all that unfounded.

"How long have you been with Shield?" she asked Luke, curious.

"About five years."

"Almost since the beginning."

"Roman and I go way back."

Natalie had met Roman DeHart and interacted with him a few times. She remembered him as a little intimidating, his eyes dark and intense, always serious and professional when she'd observed him. There'd never been any doubt in her mind that her dad had hired the best private security company around. Luke's performance so far had only solidified her judgment.

"I'm surprised I've never met you."

"Spent the first three years as a security engineer before training under Roman as a bodyguard. Now I just work for Shield on a contract basis. Trying to get a community center off the ground in my old neighborhood in Cherry Hill."

"What kind of community center?" Natalie asked, her interest piqued.

Streetlights cast shadows through the cab, and Luke shifted in his seat to face her. "A place where kids can come after school for help with homework, pickup basketball games, a free meal. I'd like to get some small group Bible studies started, too. And eventually literacy and parenting classes. Things like that."

She barely knew him, but she was immediately rooting for his success. The sincerity in his expression and the determined tone of his voice spoke to the immeasurable time he had likely poured into planning. "It sounds amazing. And like a lot of work."

"It'll be worth every dollar and every second I sink into it."

There was a story there. She didn't have a chance to ask about it because the cruiser was pulling up to the hospital entrance. Time to get her shoulder patched up and then head to the police station. Neither task appealed to her, but she wasn't a complainer, and she'd do what needed to be done, like she always did.

Luke paced the floor, silently strategizing his next steps as Natalie's shoulder got stitched up.

"Feel free to wait outside," Natalie said wryly. "I'm sure I'll be safe enough in here."

"Trying to get rid of me?" He leaned against the wall, sending her a sympathetic grin. She seemed unfazed by the needle moving in and out of her skin, the clenched fists in her lap the only sign of her discomfort.

"Maybe," she admitted. "I'm not keen on having a needle poked through my flesh. The thought of a stranger watching it happen thrills me even less."

"I'm not watching the needle," he said, his gaze never wavering from hers as the doctor shot more painkiller into the area around the knife wound. Come to think of it, her sun-kissed skin had paled, her breathing shallow.

"Some vacation, huh?" Luke asked, hoping to get her mind off the procedure.

"Not exactly what I had in mind."

"What did you have in mind?"

"I'm sure my father filled you in—a romantic honeymoon with the man who was supposed to love me. You know, until death do us part and all that." She pressed her lips together as if regretting the words. "I'm sure you don't want to hear all the sordid details."

He wouldn't mind hearing the sordid details, but he wouldn't press her for more. "I'm sorry," he offered quietly. "One-sided love hurts."

He knew that all too well. Had learned it first as a young kid, desperately trying to convince his mom to get help, to change, to love him and his siblings more than she loved her addictions and her dysfunctional romantic relationships. And the theme had repeated itself in his life more than once.

"It's hard to come to terms with the idea that it was one-sided."

He read confusion in her eyes, and it was clear that she had been blindsided by her fiancé's wedding-day abandonment. He had the urge to tell her all the things he knew she wouldn't want to hear—that she was better off without the jerk, that she had a lot going for her in life, that the right person for her would show up when she least expected him. But he had a feeling that any words he offered would come across as useless platitudes.

"All done," the doctor said, drawing back. "Eight stitches."

"Not bad." Luke offered Natalie a hand as she sat up.

She straightened, but her grip on Luke's hand felt weak. He slid an arm behind her back for more support as the doctor reviewed care instructions for the wound and then opened the door for them. As Natalie's feet met the ground, Luke held her arm, steadying her.

"I'm okay," she said, but leaned into the help he offered.

The doctor said goodbye and gestured down the hall to the exit.

"If you want to go back to the hotel, we can go to the station tomorrow," Luke suggested as he led Natalie to the checkout desk. He recognized the exhaustion setting in, along with the shock from the night's events, and didn't want to keep pushing her.

But Natalie shook her head, determined. "Let's just get it over with."

More than an hour later, Luke and Natalie had finally been fingerprinted and then escorted to the lobby of the police station, where Officer Perez was waiting to transport them back to the hotel. A storm had set in, rain pouring in windy sheets outside the ancient building. The squad car was less than thirty yards from the station's entrance, but they were all drenched by the time they reached it.

Officer Perez opened a back-passenger door and ges-

tured for them to slide in just as someone called to him
in Spanish from the far edge of the lot. Luke followed
Natalie into the car, peering across the seat and out into
the dark parking lot, where a car with flashing hazards
was parked at an odd angle with its hood popped.

"A moment, please," Officer Perez said, closing the
door and jogging away from the cruiser. Luke watched
the officer run through the downpour until he disappeared behind the open hood of the car. Normally, he'd
get out and offer some help, but the safest place for Natalie was in this car, and he didn't plan on leaving her alone.

Now was probably a good time to bring Roman up to
speed. He wouldn't be thrilled to start his Sunday with
this news, but he'd be unhappier still if Luke delayed re-
porting it.

"I'm giving my boss a call," he told Natalie, pulling
up Roman's number on his phone.

"Luke," Roman answered on the second ring, his voice
alert. "Everything okay? I was just about to call you."

"I've got things under control," Luke assured Roman,
surprised at the edge in his boss's voice. "Natalie's safe.
But we've run into a problem." He proceeded to fill Roman
in on all that had transpired that night and their plan moving forward. "As soon as we get her passport, we'll re-
schedule our return flights," he added.

"My crew's already getting the jet ready," Roman said.
"I don't want her traveling on a commercial flight when
we don't know who this guy is."

Luke leaned forward, pressed the phone closer to his
ear. The connection wasn't great, but he was pretty sure
he'd heard Roman correctly. "You're already loading up?
How did you know we—"

"There've been some developments here," Roman cut
in, his voice deadly serious. "Natalie's ex, Kyle Paxton,

is MIA. And the State police want to bring Natalie in for questioning."

"Hold on a minute," Luke said. "I'm putting you on speaker. Natalie's here with me. It's probably better if she hears the news firsthand."

What news? she mouthed, her brow furrowed.

"Natalie, how are you holding up?" Roman asked.

"I've been better, but Luke's taking good care of me," she responded, her voice tense. "What's going on, Roman?"

"Kyle is missing," he said bluntly.

"What…?" She shook her head, disbelief in her expression.

"His parents were the last people to see him, the morning of the wedding," Roman said. "When he didn't show up at the church, his parents drove back to his town house. The place had been torn up."

"Torn up?" she asked faintly.

"Ransacked. Car's missing, too."

Natalie was silent, bewilderment written all over her face.

"Have you heard from him?"

"Nothing but a text saying he couldn't go through with the wedding. He was sorry. That was it. What are the police thinking?"

"They don't have much information yet. They're anxious to speak to you."

"I'm not sure what I have to add to the conversation."

"You're the closest person to Kyle," Roman pointed out. "Any information you can offer will help the investigation."

"We'll get the passport as soon as we can, and I'll get her on the plane home," Luke said.

"Keep me posted."

Roman disconnected, and Luke shoved the phone back in his pocket.

Next to him, concern darkened Natalie's eyes, her hands clenched together in her lap. Then she dropped her gaze, whether in grief or fear, Luke couldn't tell. Her short blond waves hid her profile.

He was quiet for a moment, allowing her time to process the news. Meanwhile, his thoughts raced ahead. He didn't believe for one minute that Kyle's disappearance was random and unrelated to the attack on Natalie. But what was the connection? He didn't have much background on Kyle—only that he was a public criminal defense lawyer. Could he have made a dangerous enemy? Or was Kyle the enemy? Could he have trashed his own apartment before pulling a disappearing act? Maybe, if he had something to hide. But how did Natalie fit into the equation?

"Kyle showed up for the rehearsal dinner, right?" Luke asked her finally.

"Yes," she said without looking up, her voice tired.

"Did he seem like himself?"

She shrugged. "I guess. He was tired, but we both were. It'd been a long week with our jobs and the wedding prep."

"Did he go straight home after the dinner?"

"There was a bachelor party. He said he'd rather go home and get a good night's sleep before the wedding, but he didn't want to let the guys down."

"Do you know where they went? Who he was with?"

"A restaurant and bar in Fells Point. Just his groomsmen. It would have been a pretty tame group."

Luke was skeptical about the idea of a tame group of young men at a bar in Fells Point on a Friday night, but decided to keep that thought to himself.

"What about the past few weeks leading up to the wedding? Was he acting differently at all?"

Natalie sighed and shifted in her seat, tugging the seat belt away from her injured shoulder. "Not that I noticed. But, like I said, we had a lot going on."

She still hadn't met his eyes, and Luke suspected she was withholding details she didn't want to share.

"He certainly wasn't acting strange enough for me to suspect he planned to call the wedding off," she added.

"When did you get the text?"

"Yesterday morning. Fifteen minutes before the ceremony."

Natalie rubbed the back of her neck with both hands. Frustration? Grief? She finally let her hands drop and turned to look Luke in the eyes. "It was bizarre," she said, and there was fire in her eyes. "I mean, he had all the opportunity in the world to call things off the night before, and all morning, too—but to wait until just before the ceremony…"

Her thoughts echoed Luke's, but they couldn't do much in the way of investigating until they got back stateside.

"Did anyone else see him that morning?"

"I don't know. He was supposed to meet up with his groomsmen and drive to the church together. They showed up without him, and no one mentioned to me he wouldn't be coming."

"How many groomsmen? And how well do you know them?"

"Three, and not that well. His college buddy, Trent. A cousin named Lee. And you probably know his friend Jordan—he works at Shield?"

"He could be a good source when we get back."

A form finally emerged from behind the car across the lot, and Officer Perez jogged back in their direction, his head down as he slogged through the heavy rain.

The driver's door opened and the officer climbed in without a glance back, his hair dripping, his tan uniform soaked to a dark brown. He started up the car and pulled out of the lot in a hurry, wheels skidding along wet pavement.

Next to Luke, Natalie grabbed on to the side of the door to keep herself from sliding across the seat into him, and sudden alarm fired up his adrenaline.

The interior of the vehicle was all dark shadows, the man's face indistinguishable in the rearview, but when they passed under a lone street lamp, Luke knew they were in trouble. Officer Perez wasn't driving the cruiser.

The driver was young and clean-shaven—and clearly on some sort of mission. Luke considered the possibility that Perez had traded out with another officer—maybe a rookie with a chip on his shoulder? He did appear to be wearing the uniform...

But something wasn't right, and as the vehicle climbed a winding hill, wipers slashing against sheets of rain, he tried to take stock of the situation. Luke didn't know the terrain, but he did know they hadn't even once traveled downhill, and the route wasn't familiar.

"Excuse me, Officer," he said, as if he hadn't realized what had happened.

The driver glanced in the rearview mirror, but said nothing.

"I think we might have missed a turn back there," Luke said. "We're staying at the Riu de Sueños."

"Road is blocked," the guy answered gruffly, his accent thick. The road ahead curved sharply left, but the man barely slowed, taking the corner hard. Natalie slid into Luke's side, her hand bracing against the seat in front of her.

"Hey, we're not in a hurry. Take it easy," Luke said,

forcing his voice to sound relaxed even as their reality became alarmingly clear: the cruiser had been carjacked.

The man let up on the gas, the whites of his eyes flashing in the rearview mirror.

"Right, right," he said.

Visibility was low, the dim glow of the car's headlights fighting with the heavy rain. It was an older model cruiser, with thick cage wiring separating the back seat from the driver. No way to get to the driver, and it would be too dangerous to try to stop the car, anyway.

They didn't have many options out here, but if he waited too much longer, getting back down the mountain would be difficult. If they escaped now, they could take cover in the trees, call for help.

He tapped Natalie's finger to get her attention. "Follow my lead," he whispered. Then loud enough for the driver to hear, "Natalie, are you okay? You don't look so good."

Her brow furrowed, but she caught on. "No," she said, her hands coming to her abdomen. "I…feel sick."

"We need to pull over for a minute," Luke said to the driver.

"Okay. Next place I find."

Natalie moaned next to Luke, clutching her stomach.

"We can't wait," Luke insisted. "Pull over *now*!"

But the car didn't slow, confirming Luke's suspicions that their driver was on a mission—and it wasn't to get them safely back to the hotel.

Natalie glanced at him, her expression giving way to fear. Then she put her hand to her mouth. "I think I'm about to be sick!" she said, and doubled over.

"Pull over!" Luke yelled to the driver. "She needs to get out!"

Natalie moaned loudly, and the driver finally swerved to the right and slammed on the brakes. They pitched forward, both throwing out their arms to keep from hitting the seats in front of them. The driver unlocked the car, glancing at them in the mirror, but not turning back.

Maybe he thought he'd fooled them. That they hadn't noticed he'd switched places with Perez. Luke would use that to his advantage if he could.

Luke nodded to Natalie, and she didn't hesitate.

She yanked on the handle and jumped out of the car, running behind a thick copse of trees, out of sight. Luke scooted to the door, planting his feet on the wet ground and waiting for the driver to make a move. With Natalie safely out of harm's way, he'd have a better shot at taking the guy down. He watched the driver in his periphery, saw him shift in his seat. Getting a weapon? Luke didn't have any weapons, but he would be ready. He shifted to the edge of the seat, keeping his peripheral vision on the driver.

But the driver didn't make a move.

Luke considered his options. If the driver thought he still had them fooled, that could buy them some time. Making a run for it may be a safer option than confronting a potentially armed criminal in the middle of nowhere. If Luke got taken down, Natalie would be on her own.

"I'll just go check on her," Luke said, making his decision and emerging from the vehicle into the pouring rain.

He quickly covered the ground between the car and the foliage Natalie had disappeared behind and found her crouched by a thick tree trunk. "Let's move," Luke whispered, grasping her hand and leading her deeper into the thick forest. They treaded quietly, low to the ground, the echo of rain eating up any sound they made.

Luke figured they had about a minute or two before the guy came looking, but he overestimated. They'd barely covered twenty yards when a voice echoed too close.

"Hey!"

Natalie's hand tightened on Luke's and they picked

up their pace. Luke didn't think they'd been seen, but he couldn't be sure.

A thin beam of light shone into the forest, just missing them as Luke pulled Natalie behind a massive fallen tree.

"Stay here."

He started to leave, but she grabbed his arm. "What are you doing?" she whispered.

"My job." He pried her hand off his arm. "Stay low and don't move from this spot."

Leaving her there, Luke circled back toward the road. If he could stay out of the guy's view, he could take him by surprise, turn the tables on him.

It didn't take him long to spot the man, his dark figure plunging forward into the woods, his flashlight moving in an organized search pattern. Luke ducked behind a thick patch of shrubs, watching the beam of light track for them. What was this guy's game? And what had happened to Officer Perez? Were the police somehow involved in the crimes against Natalie? That seemed far-fetched, but he couldn't discount the idea. He waited for the flashlight beam to pass by him again before continuing. His approach would have to be timed perfectly. He wouldn't do Natalie any good lying dead in the middle of the woods.

The beam of light stopped, backtracked.

Homed in on the heavy fallen tree Natalie was hiding behind.

Luke's hands clenched into fists, praying Natalie's cover hadn't been blown.

But footsteps sloshed closer, louder, faster. He peered around the edge of the shrubs, saw the man heading straight for Natalie's location—flashlight in one hand, gun in the other.

She'd been seen.

THREE

Natalie's heart pounded, her hands grasping on to the damp rough trunk she crouched behind. Rain ran down her face. She ignored it. The heavy thud of footsteps stamped closer along soggy brush.

Peering over the edge of the trunk, she tried to gauge his location.

A beam of light and a dark shadow was heading directly toward her hiding place. Her breath caught in her throat and she pushed herself up. Now or never. She had to run.

She swiveled away from the trunk, cold mud catching her sandals as she half ran, half slid along the edge of an embankment. Could she slip over to the other side for cover? It was too dark to see how steep the drop was. Better not risk it. Branches scraped her arms, rain clouding her vision. Beyond her own harsh breaths and the squall of the storm, she could hear nothing. But a glimmer of light flashed across her face, and she knew he was close.

Where was Luke? She strained forward, head down against the pelting rain. But her foot hit a slippery patch of underbrush, and she went down, ribs smacking against hard earth. Natalie raked in a hollow breath, stunned by the impact.

She tried to push herself up, her breath ragged, her body drenched. She had to keep moving, but she was losing the battle. Clawing at the slick forest floor, she desperately tried to right herself again, anticipating the coming attack.

But no attack came.

The footsteps vanished.

The light dropped away.

Natalie turned, hope rising again as she saw Luke and the attacker wrestling in a heap just yards behind her. The flashlight had landed on the ground nearby, and renewed strength surged as she backtracked, snatching it up and turning it toward the pair. Maybe if Luke could see what he was doing…

"Get back!" Luke yelled as she aimed the light on the pair. "He's got a gun!"

The gun glimmered under the light as the assailant twisted, furiously trying to aim the weapon at Luke. But Luke was stronger, his grip fastened on the man's gun arm, bending his wrist back until the weapon dropped to the wet ground.

In seconds, Luke had the guy on his stomach, his arms pinned, Luke's knee to his back.

Sirens sounded nearby. Had the police tracked the car? Natalie hoped so. The impostor continued to struggle, and the wet landscape made Luke's job more difficult. Natalie's gaze caught on the discarded gun and she reached down and grabbed it.

"Stay down!" she yelled, training the weapon on the carjacker.

He stilled, and Natalie consciously slowed her breathing, the gun slick and heavy in her palm as the sirens grew louder. She hadn't touched a gun in years, ever since the concealed handgun license class her father had pushed her to take. She'd borrowed a friend's gun for the class because she had never intended to own one herself. She might rethink that decision when she got home.

Lights flashed red and blue through the trees as police cars pulled up next to the abandoned cruiser at the edge of the street. Officers filed out of cars, swarming toward them in the woods, guns drawn. Flashlights flooded the scene, dark figures closing in on them. Relief flooded over Natalie. Help had arrived.

But as the officers drew closer, seeds of alarm took root. They were yelling toward the trio in Spanish. A command, it seemed. A hostile command.

"Do you know what they're saying?"

Luke's eyes met hers. "Drop the gun. Hands in the air."

"But—"

"Drop your weapon!" someone repeated in English this time.

"Do it," Luke said. "They don't know the situation."

Slowly, carefully, she set the gun down as far away from the thug as she could reach without moving her feet. She scanned the scene as she straightened. Five officers. No, six.

"On the ground!" someone yelled as the officers drew closer in a staggered formation.

The heat of the situation didn't lend itself to explanations. Especially with six guns aimed at them.

Luke moved off the thug and put his hands up, lowering himself to his knees. Natalie followed his lead, slow, cautious, keeping her hands up.

But then suddenly, the assailant pushed himself up from the ground and took off.

Guns fired and shouts erupted, and Luke dove over Natalie to give her cover. "Stay down!"

Shattered Trust

He covered her for mere seconds before his weight lifted off her and he was dragged away by an officer.

"Keep your hands where they can see them!" Luke yelled to Natalie as another officer grabbed her arm and yanked her up.

She could hardly believe what was happening as handcuffs were secured and they were led together to a police car. Was this some kind of a setup? Why were they being arrested? What did the police think they had done?

Luke said something in Spanish to the officer at his side, but the man made no response as they were escorted to a waiting squad car and locked in like criminals.

Natalie looked at Luke, lights from the other cars flashing on his face. "What just happened?"

He shook his head. "Your guess is as good as mine."

He radiated tension, every muscle on alert as they waited—cuffed and soaking wet—to find out what would happen next.

He cast an assessing gaze over her, and she willed away the tremor of aftershock that had started to take hold.

"We'll get out of here soon," he said.

"You don't know that."

Luke didn't respond, and Natalie's pulse clamored against rising anxiety. Luke had managed to protect her up until this point, but neither of them had any control now. Her gaze strayed out the window toward the dark hill where the officers had spread out in search of the suspect. What was he after? Why pursue the chase? Why go to such great lengths to get to her? He had a gun. He'd been close. He could have easily shot her, but he hadn't. On the other hand, he'd fought hard to turn his gun on Luke.

"What's this guy's game?" Natalie asked, thinking out loud. "A human trafficking scheme?"

"It's possible."

"But why go to such great lengths? Don't traffickers spend time luring their victims? Or kidnapping easy prey?"

Luke nodded. "I agree. It doesn't seem to fit. More likely a kidnap for ransom—if he knows your dad's wealthy."

"How would he know that, though?"

"Good point… Plus, the ransacked hotel room makes me think he's after something you have."

"Well, he got the pearl necklace. But he probably didn't know I had it, and I doubt he knew its value."

"Even if he did, I'm not sure a twelve-hundred-dollar necklace would be temptation enough for this scheme. You didn't bring anything else of value with you? Something you might not have been thinking about with all the chaos back at the hotel?"

"Nothing but my engagement ring."

"You still wearing it?"

"I put it on my necklace chain when I changed earlier."

"Interesting."

She shrugged. "Seemed like the safest place for it, all things considered. It was either that or toss it in the ocean."

"I'm surprised you didn't. No one would have blamed you."

"It didn't seem practical," she said simply.

"Do you always do the practical thing?"

"Pretty much. Up until yesterday morning, anyhow."

Luke nodded his understanding.

"How much is the ring worth?"

"I never saw the bill, but Kyle said he had it insured for six grand, so under that. Doesn't seem like enough to warrant all…*this*." She looked pointedly around the inside of the cruiser and wriggled her cuffed hands. Her arms were achy, the metal digging into her wrists. "Why arrest us?" Even as she asked the question, her mind traced back over the night's events, horror washing down her spine as the pieces started to come together. "What do you think happened to Officer Perez back at the station?"

Luke's lips flattened into a grim line as another officer approached the cruiser. "I have a feeling we're about to find out."

The officer rounded the front of the car and slipped into the driver's seat, not even sparing them a glance. "I will transport you to the station," he said as he started the car and pulled onto the road, lights still flashing.

"We're American citizens," Luke explained. "This is all a misunderstanding. The one you're after is the one who ran."

At that, the officer glanced at him in the rearview, his eyes black with barely controlled emotion. "An officer was killed tonight. You will be interviewed."

Natalie shut her eyes and leaned back into the seat, ignoring the handcuffs pressing into her lower back.

Had their assailant followed them from the hotel, waited in the lot to distract Officer Perez—then incapacitated him? Murdered him?

She shuddered at the thought, and unexpected tears welled up as she thought about the kindhearted Officer Perez. He'd worn a wedding ring. Tonight, his wife was a widow. Did they have children? Grandchildren? It wasn't lost on Natalie that his life had been taken while pursuing her protection. As much as she wanted to get out of Mexico, she hoped the murderer would be caught and brought to justice first.

By the time they'd answered questions at the police station and been escorted back to the hotel, they'd missed breakfast and it was high time for lunch. This was the last place Luke wanted to be, but for now, it was the most practical and probably the safest. The police had shot and killed the man who had murdered Officer Perez and carjacked the cruiser, identifying him as a member of a local gang. But the man on the beach and the man who had killed Perez were two different people. Luke was sure of it, and he couldn't take any chances with Natalie in public. Unfortunately, they would need to stay out of sight for a while. Natalie's father had friends in high places, but even he couldn't pull enough strings for someone to meet them at the consulate's office on a Sunday morning to fix the passport problem. They'd have to go first thing in the morning.

Luke's hotel room adjoined Natalie's, but he would be spending the night on the couch in her room, keeping watch. Since it was an interior room on the seventh floor, there was no balcony to be concerned about, which was a good thing. Natalie had headed straight to the shower when they'd arrived, and Luke had ordered room service. They couldn't very well sit out in plain view in the hotel restaurant.

Luke glanced at the clock. Not quite 1:30 p.m. He ran a hand through his still-damp hair and started a pot of coffee. He hated the stuff, but fatigue was setting in, and today promised to be a long day of waiting.

Seemed like his entire life had been a lesson in waiting. Waiting for his mother to finish another detox program. Waiting for the courts to find a foster home willing to take all three Everett siblings. Waiting for the next mealtime and hoping there'd be food. He still didn't have much tolerance for waiting, but somewhere in his early teens, when he and his siblings had been separated for the third time in as many months, he'd learned how to manage the anxiety that rose up during those long periods of uncertainty. He prayed, and he fought for a semblance of control by taking action.

He didn't feel in control right now, though, and his hands were tied, which was a problem. In a foreign country, without backup and without an option of immediate escape, Luke was the sole protector of Natalie's life. Even as the weight of his responsibility settled on his shoulders, he caught himself falling into old patterns of fear. He was not Natalie's sole protector, he reminded himself. She had a protector far greater than Luke or an entire team of Shield bodyguards.

He closed his eyes briefly and recited a prayer of protection over his client. Luke would do his job, and he had to trust that God would take care of the rest.

A knock came at the door, and he peered through the peephole, watching as a room service attendant took the note Luke had propped on the door handle. Inside, he'd left a tip and instructions to leave the trays in the hallway. The attendant pocketed the tip and set the two trays to the right of the door, then continued down the hall with the cart until she was out of sight.

He waited a full minute after the attendant left and then cracked the door open, surveying the silent hallway.

Seeing no one, he quickly moved both trays into the room and bolted the door again. The scent of grilled steak and rice slowed his adrenaline, and he set the trays on the coffee table next to the couch, listening to the shower and wondering just how long Natalie planned to be in there.

Not a minute later, as he weighed his growing hunger against the rudeness of eating without her, the shower stopped.

"Food's here," he called through the door.

"Be right there."

Luke poured coffee and forced himself to drink it while he waited for Natalie to appear. He didn't have to wait long. Within two minutes, she opened the door, steam filtering into the room.

"I feel so much better," she said as she walked out, still toweling her hair. She'd changed into a pair of black Nike shorts and a gray V-neck T-shirt, and she smiled apologetically at him, clearly refreshed. "I think there's still hot water left for you."

"I'll wait till later," Luke said, wondering what it was about her that seemed even more beautiful now than he'd noticed before.

Her attention strayed to the trays on the table. "You didn't have to wait for me," she said. "If I had known, I wouldn't have spent five years in the shower."

Luke laughed at that. "It was hardly five years. Anyhow, after what we just survived, I figured we should celebrate together with breakfast."

"Agreed," Natalie said with a small smile, sitting down on one side of the couch. "Let's eat."

Luke pulled a chair up to the opposite side of the table and bent his head in a quick silent prayer. When he opened his eyes, Natalie was scooping rice onto a tortilla, but her gaze flicked up to him, curious. If she had a question, she didn't ask it. Instead, she turned to the topic of the weekend.

They tossed ideas back and forth about how the beach attacker and the carjacker may have been related, but neither had a solid theory.

"I can't help but think Kyle's somehow connected to all this," Luke finally said, venturing into the hypothesis he hadn't dared mention before.

Natalie frowned and set down her fork. "How? I don't see it."

"The timing, for one," he said carefully, aware that he was treading into deep waters. "Out of the blue, he cancels the wedding. Then disappears. And on the same day, you're stalked, attacked twice and robbed." He watched her expression, but couldn't read it.

"I see your point, but what motive would he have?"

"You'd know that better than I would."

She continued eating, but her movements were stiff, her demeanor suddenly closed. She'd spoken a handful of sentences about her relationship with Kyle, and seemed determined to keep her emotions and thoughts on the matter close to her heart.

They ate in silence, but Luke was no longer hungry. The air in the room had gone cold, Natalie clearly lost in thoughts she didn't plan to make Luke privy to. That bothered him. If she wanted the best protection, she needed to commit to full disclosure. Luke had never been one to let frustration fester, so he finally placed the tin cover back over his plate.

"You know, Natalie, my job is to protect you. I can't do that to the best of my ability if you're keeping things from me."

Her eyebrows raised as if she was offended by his assumption. "I'm hardly keeping things from you," she said, too politely.

The politeness bothered him more than her silence, and he recognized it as a defense mechanism. She didn't want to share the details of her personal life, but while Luke could respect a desire for privacy, he couldn't afford to spend time tiptoeing around the questions he had.

"Then tell me more about your relationship with Kyle," he said. "Start there."

Natalie wiped her mouth with a napkin before meeting Luke's eyes again. "I don't see how telling you about Kyle will help you protect me."

"Every detail helps fill in the big picture," he explained. "Trust me. And if you can't trust me, then humor me."

She sighed, and he knew he'd convinced her. Not saying another word, he waited for her to decide where to start and how much to share.

Once she began, she didn't tell him much that he didn't already know. Kyle was a lawyer slogging through his first years of practicing, an aspiring politician who had interned with Natalie's father several years ago. That's how they'd met—through Natalie's father. They held many common interests and hit it off right away. The relationship just naturally progressed to a marriage proposal.

Those words struck Luke as odd—too formal to describe how a friendship had transformed into marriage-material love. He filed that information away and continued to listen as Natalie described how life had been a whirlwind since the New Year's gala at her father's estate. Kyle had been busy and distant at times, but she'd attributed it to the stress of planning the wedding and his heavy workload.

"I didn't actually think much of it until a few months ago," Natalie said. "He'd had a bad couple of weeks. Lost his phone, got in a fender bender, missed an important meeting at work. He just seemed out of sorts. Then one night I was going through my bills, and I opened a credit card statement I didn't recognize. It had my name on it, but I didn't own the credit card."

"What were the charges?"

Natalie turned her palms up and gestured around the room. "This vacation. Kyle had applied for the card in my name without even talking to me about it."

Now *that* was news he might be able to use. Any

time someone started talking about finances new motives came into play.

"He said the new card came with bonus points and he got our airfare free."

"Why not just apply in his name?"

"He already had one in his name. The points were for new cardholders."

"Hmm."

She shrugged. "It almost made sense, except for the fact that he didn't ask me first."

It didn't make any sense to Luke, and it screamed to him that Kyle may not have been as well off as he had perhaps claimed to be.

"In hindsight, though, I should have broken things off then. He really lost his temper that night. I'd never seen him so angry."

"The way I see it, you were the only one who had a reason to be angry," Luke said, trying to follow her story.

"I *was* angry. I realized I'd never received a new credit card in the mail, and I asked if he'd intercepted it so I wouldn't find out what he'd done. That's what set him off. Said if I was so suspicious about his motives, maybe we shouldn't be getting married." Her already sun-kissed skin turned a deeper pink. So this was the piece she hadn't wanted to share.

"I should have taken him up on that," she added.

"But you didn't."

"He apologized almost as soon as the words were out of his mouth. It didn't happen again. But the memory stuck." Her eyes were glossy, and she looked down at her tray, setting the cover on top of her plate. "And there are your details," she added softly.

"How do you—"

"I'm sorry, Luke," Natalie interrupted before he could

ask how she thought Kyle was doing financially. "Can we discuss this more later? I'm exhausted."

"Sure," he said easily, even though he would have much rather pressed on. "We could both use some rest."

"Thanks," she said, her tone a little surprised, as if she'd expected him to argue with her.

He would have, but he sensed that wasn't the way to gain Natalie's trust, so instead he stood and picked up the trays, walking them to the door and setting them outside in the hallway to be retrieved. After double-checking the dead bolt and flipping the latch lock, he piled a couple throw pillows on one side of the couch and sprawled out there, his back to the side of the room where Natalie had already pulled back the covers on her bed and switched off the small lamp on the nightstand. Behind him, her covers rustled for a few seconds as she settled in for a nap.

It wasn't long before the steady sound of her breathing signaled that she was asleep. Despite the coffee, fatigue was taking over for Luke, as well. No way would he be able to stay awake. But there was also no way anyone would get into the room without bulldozing the door, so Luke sent a quick text to Roman to check into Kyle's finances, and then he let his eyes close so he could get some rest, too.

The blast of an alarm woke him, and Luke shot up on the couch, momentarily disoriented before realizing the fire alarm was going off. Jumping to his feet, he flipped on lights and turned to wake Natalie, but she was already out of bed and shoving her shoes on. Luke glanced at the clock in the room. They'd slept almost six hours. He grabbed his backpack, mentally running through the hotel exits as adrenaline flushed away the deep sleep he'd just woken from. There were two sets of stairs on their wing, and two more on the opposite wing. And if all else failed, a fire escape could be accessed just around the corner.

"Let's go," he said, leading the way to the door as a recorded evacuation announcement began to blare over the alarm.

He touched the door handle. No heat. Unbolting the lock, he swung the door open before a thought struck him. He hesitated in the doorway, and Natalie came up behind him. People filtered out of their rooms, hurrying to nearby stairwells.

"What's wrong?" Natalie asked.

He backed into the room and locked the door again.

"I know you're the security expert here, but I don't want to get trapped on the seventh floor with a fire," Natalie said, raising her voice over the piercing alarm.

"What if there is no fire?"

Natalie looked at him skeptically.

"Doesn't this seem like too much at once?" he asked. "I'm not leading you into a trap."

"I don't know, Luke." Her frantic eyes flicked to the door. "I say we take our chances and evacuate."

He hesitated, but his instincts told him he was right.

"Let me check it out," he said. "I'll be five minutes, tops. You stay here. Bolt the door. If I see any sign of smoke, we'll evacuate."

"No way. Five minutes could be life or death." She crossed the room to reach for the door, and he followed her, his hand coming to her arm.

"Wait, Natalie. Trust me on this. Stay by the phone. If something happens, I'll call you. The fire escape is at the end of the hall, to the right. But I'll be back before you need it."

Natalie didn't look convinced, but she nodded. "Five minutes."

"Five minutes. Bolt the door. Stay by the phone."

He stepped into the hallway and stayed until he heard the bolt click into place, then ran down the near-empty hall to do a quick circuit of the seventh floor. He checked the fire escape to make sure it was accessible, then raced down to each floor below, peeking into the hallways and seeing no sign of fire or even smoke.

As the lobby came into view, it became apparent to Luke that his suspicion was right. It was a false alarm. Whether a drill, a malfunction or a trap, he didn't know. But he'd passed the five-minute mark, and it was time to head back up to the room. He started to text Natalie that he was on his way back up, when his phone rang in his hand. A local number. He swiped to answer, but he was already sprinting up the stairs when he heard Natalie's voice, and his entire body went cold.

"Luke! Hurry! He's here!"

FOUR

Natalie dropped the phone back on the receiver and eyed the door. The handle was still, no longer jostling up and down by the hands of whoever stood on the other side. Had he left? She'd nearly let the guy in seconds ago when he'd scanned a key card and tried the handle. Assuming Luke had returned, Natalie had reached to unlock the dead bolt, checking the peephole as an afterthought— and froze. A stranger stood outside her door, clad in a hotel uniform.

She strained to listen for movement from the hallway, but could hear nothing above the ear-piercing fire alarm. He couldn't get inside. She knew that. He'd need an override card for the dead bolt, and then he'd have to get around the thick metal door latch. Still, Natalie wasn't one to stand around helplessly hoping for the best. She dragged the love seat toward the entryway, shoving it against the door for good measure. And then the dead bolt slid open.

She gasped, darting away from the door and grabbing the heavy leather chair from the sitting room. She hefted it onto the love seat just as the door slammed inches into the room, the sofa sliding forward as the door met the last bit of resistance—the four-inch metal latch that seconds ago had given Natalie a false sense of security.

She flipped the coffee table on its side, dragging it over to add to the furniture fortress as the door banged violently against the latch, the intruder slamming against it repeatedly. If Luke didn't make it back in time…

Racing to the nightstand, she tried to reach security again, waiting with growing panic as the door frame around the latch began to splinter. A busy signal still, the evacuation announcement only minutes old. Screws popped out of place, the latch giving way. Natalie dropped the phone. The furniture would slow him down, but she needed a weapon.

She searched the room, tossing the shade from a lamp and cracking the edge of the bulb against the nightstand. Grabbing the wrought iron base in one hand, she raced to Luke's adjoining door. She jammed the handle up and down, knowing it was futile because Luke had never even entered his assigned room. The door was locked from the other side.

One final thud hit her door, the latch breaking away from the frame with a splitting crack. Natalie bit back a scream, gripping her makeshift weapon with all her strength, willing herself to stand her ground as the door pressed solidly, inch by inch, against the pile of furniture. This couldn't be happening. But it was. A hand snaked into the room, connecting with the top of the chair and shoving it off the pile.

Natalie crept toward the door, positioning herself out of sight, preparing to either fight or make a run for it.

Then a loud shout came from down the hall, and the gloved hand retreated. Natalie stood stock-still, hearing nothing over the still-wailing alarm and her own thunderous heartbeat.

Long seconds passed, and then minutes, and she stood rooted to her spot, her attention fixed on the door, her imagination running wild. What if Luke needed help?

Maybe she should push through the furniture and go out there. But if the intruder was gone, he could come back at any moment. And what if an accomplice was heading toward the room right now?

The fire alarm suddenly shut off, but the ringing in her ears continued as she strained to hear other sounds from the hallway. Nothing. That was it. She wasn't going to stay cornered in the room, waiting for the unknown with no escape route except for the broken door.

She started toward the mess she'd made, but jumped back when a rap sounded at the door.

"It's me."

Luke!

He peered into the gap between the door and the wall, eyeing the furniture.

"I'll come through my room," he said, and disappeared from view.

She hurried to the adjoining door, mere seconds passing before Luke unlocked his side and rushed into her room.

"Are you okay?" He stepped close to her, his gaze assessing.

She nodded, because she couldn't find her voice. Relief clogged her throat.

"Here." Luke reached out and took the lamp stand from her. She hadn't realized she'd still been holding it. He set it on the floor, then straightened, his hands coming to her arms as if to steady her. Come to think of it, she was a little shaky on her feet.

"I'm sorry."

Natalie wasn't sure what to make of the apology. He'd made it back in time, after all. She opened her mouth to point that out, but then his hands slid down her arms and slipped around her waist, tugging her close.

Her breath caught at the gesture, and for a moment her guard came down, her arms wrapping around his waist, her cheek resting against his chest as she listened to the beat of his heart—strong and somehow reassuring. They stood motionless like that for long seconds as Natalie's tension fled, exchanged for the unexpected flood of connection. She should step away now, but his hands smoothed circles along her lower back and she closed her eyes instead, suddenly aware of the solid wall of his chest beneath his soft T-shirt, the faint scent of his cologne, the warmth of his breath tickling her ear.

"I thought it was a trap. I shouldn't have left you here."

His words pulled her back to reality and back to her senses. Natalie let her hands drop away, and he followed suit, taking a small step back.

"It could have been a trap," Natalie reasoned. For all they knew, someone else had been waiting outside. "You're only one person." One highly trained, entirely too-good-looking person. Her senses still reeled from the warmth of his hands and the unexpected comfort in his embrace. Comfort and chemistry, if she was honest.

A cold realization washed over her. Maybe her sister had been right. Maybe Natalie was afraid of being alone. What other explanation could there be for her increasing attraction to a man she'd met only yesterday, just hours after her wedding was supposed to have taken place?

"We need to get moving." Luke was already packing his belongings into his backpack, obviously not affected one bit by the hug. "We'll find somewhere else to stay tonight. It's not safe here."

"Where did he go?" Natalie asked, her attention straying to the damaged door.

Luke folded his jacket and stuffed it into his backpack. "Fire escape. I couldn't catch up with him and look out for you at the same time. Not with that broken door. Got ahold of Canto on his cell on the way back up. His team is on the lookout."

"Which means the guy got away," Natalie said.

She stepped around Luke and entered the bathroom, gathering her toiletries into her travel bag.

"Maybe not. Security cameras probably picked up some images," Luke pointed out.

Natalie reentered the room, popping the toiletry bag into her suitcase and pulling out a pair of sneakers before zipping up her luggage. "He was wearing a hotel uniform."

"I noticed that. Could be an employee—he had access to an override key. Seems like they'll catch him. But when they do, we'll be gone."

He slung his backpack over his shoulder. "We'll need a car, which might take a bit. Let's go. My room's more secure." He grabbed the handle of Natalie's suitcase. "Got everything?"

She nodded and followed him through the adjoining door to his room, locking up behind them as Luke flipped on lights.

He rolled her suitcase out of the way and set down his backpack, pulling out a laptop and opening it at the desk. "Just relax for a few while I figure out who to call."

Natalie took the oversize leather chair in the sitting room, but she couldn't relax. Her mind searched for answers, trying to make sense of all that had happened. Not for the first time in the past twenty-four hours, anger surged—mostly at Kyle, because he was the one who had insisted on this nightmare of a honeymoon and then pulled a disappearing act. But truthfully, she was just as mad at herself.

After all, she only had herself to blame. She'd spent

years making decisions to keep the people she loved happy. Wasn't that why she still had the gaudy ring? Why more than three-hundred guests had sat waiting in the church yesterday morning instead of a small gathering of family on her dad's property? Why she was on a beach in Mexico instead of a mountain resort in Virginia?

Then again, she had to cut herself a little slack. Kyle had been, for the most part, the perfect boyfriend. He'd brought her dancing, surprised her with tickets to the theater, even picked her up one evening for a surprise road trip to a nearby ski lodge, where they'd spent a couple of hours tubing like kids and sipping hot chocolate. What they'd shared had been real, not imagined. Somewhere along the line, though, it had shifted—and she had somehow missed all the signs.

She'd been telling herself it had only been a couple of months since he'd been acting a little off, ever since March with the credit card. But if she was honest with herself, it had started earlier than that. The first time she could remember sensing something wasn't right was at the New Year's gala, when the countdown had begun and Kyle was nowhere to be found. He appeared just seconds after the New Year rang in, sweeping her into a kiss that felt theatric and tasted like alcohol. Yet, she had never questioned him. When he proposed the very next day, Natalie's concerns about the prior evening had melted away.

Funny how easy it was for her to work with clients and speak to large groups, even in front of cameras, yet she always had a hard time finding her voice in relationships—perhaps because she easily separated work from her personal life. She'd always thought it was fear of conflict that kept her quiet, but maybe it was more than that. Maybe it was fear of loss.

She was an expert peacekeeper. Had learned the art

during the years following her little brother's murder, as her family had fallen apart. The role had stuck. She far preferred it to conflict, but there should probably be a balance because somewhere along the way, she'd lost sight of who she really was and what she really wanted in life.

One week ago, she'd turned twenty-nine. Maybe it was time for a break. Time to learn to be content, even happy, in her own skin. Time to develop a sense of security without a companion by her side at all times. Time to go home after work and learn to fill the quiet with purpose instead of pouring herself into yet another relationship. The idea sounded appealingly freeing.

"Yes, Riu de Sueños," Luke was saying into his phone, jotting notes on a hotel notepad as he spoke. He must have secured a rental car. "Hold on." He set the pen down and glanced Natalie's way with a thumbs-up and a grin that shouldn't have stirred up any emotion except for relief. But relief was not what made her pulse leap, what called up the slide of his hands down her arms, what sparked her to smile back and then quickly look away. In her periphery, she saw him digging out his wallet, sliding out a credit card. As he began to read off the numbers for the rental company, Natalie reined in her wayward emotions. They couldn't be trusted. She didn't know why she kept falling into doomed relationships and holding on to them, but she refused to do it again. She'd stayed too long with her high school boyfriend, even when their lives clearly started taking different paths. Then, she'd stayed too long with her college boyfriend, even when their values collided on too many important points. And since her sister had gotten married, Natalie had been bouncing around the dating scene, rebounding from one short relationship to the next, until Kyle. Why? Was she really so afraid to be alone? The cycle had to stop. It was time for change.

Silently, she made a promise to herself. One year without a man in her life. One year to explore the independence she had always claimed she wanted. One year, she dared to vow, *alone*. The first step? Getting out of Mexico alive so she could start pursuing the life she should have started living years ago.

Luke ended the call and turned to her. "They were about to close, but I paid extra to get them to deliver a car here. Said they'll arrive within the hour."

"Where do we go from here?"

"Somewhere close to the consulate's office so we don't have far to travel in the morning. Somewhere touristy and crowded so we'll be hard to tail." He turned back to his laptop. "I'll figure it out."

She had no doubt he would. He'd already proven himself competent and capable. She hated that she wasn't contributing more. It seemed like all she'd done so far was attract danger. Silently, she ran through the questions Luke had asked her earlier about her relationship with Kyle. She regretted sharing so much of her story. Truth was, she was embarrassed that she'd ended up in a relationship—and nearly a marriage—that was fueled more by comfort, security and practicality than love.

Even so, she doubted Luke's hypothesis about Kyle's involvement here. He simply didn't have a motive. Not one that Natalie could see, anyway. The kidnapping for ransom idea—though almost as far-fetched—seemed more likely.

She pulled out her own laptop and waited impatiently for it to load, the Wi-Fi connecting far too slowly. Finally, she opened the browser, and a quick search was all she needed to add credence to the kidnapping or sex trafficking theories. The Riviera wasn't the safest place for American tourists anymore. In the past year alone, four American women had disappeared, ages nineteen to thirty-four. The youngest had eventually been recovered from a human trafficking ring. The oldest, after a failed ransom pursuit, had been found murdered. The other two remained missing. Dread settled hard as a rock in the pit of her stomach. She did not want to be victim number five.

"You okay over there?"

Natalie startled and looked up from the screen, meeting Luke's concerned gaze.

"Check this out." She picked up the laptop and walked it over to him, setting it on the desk next to his.

He scrolled through the series of articles she'd pulled up before finally closing her laptop.

"What do you think?"

"I think I've been so hooked on the idea of Kyle's involvement that I didn't even think to do a search like this. Good work. Something to keep in mind." He handed the laptop back to her. "I hope you're right."

"What?" She frowned, wondering what he could possibly mean by that.

"If you're right, we just need to make it onto that plane tomorrow afternoon and you'll be safe. If I'm right, I'll be bringing you from one danger zone to the next."

He closed his laptop and slid it into his backpack. "Either way, you'll be safer back in the States. I booked a room for the night at a busy hotel about midway between the airport and the consulate's office. The car should be here any minute. For now, our goal is to get out of here unseen and lose any tail we might pick up before we get there."

Night was descending already, along with another storm. Seemed like they were getting the worst of the rainy season, but that could work to their advantage. Darkness and rain would make them harder to follow. On the flip side, it would also make it more difficult to detect whether they were being followed.

The windshield wipers slashed furiously against sheets of rain along the fairly empty highway. As far as Luke could tell, they'd gotten out of the hotel unnoticed and hadn't picked up any followers. He hadn't even told Officer Canto they were checking out early. He'd notify him tomorrow, when they were safely on board the plane.

Luke glanced again at the fuel gauge, anxious energy thrumming in his veins. He supposed beggars couldn't be choosers, but he'd expected the car to be delivered with at least a half tank of gas. He figured the few gallons they had might get them to Cancun, but the car was old. No telling how much of a gas-guzzler it was. And the last thing they needed was to be stranded on the side of the road during a storm like this, in a foreign country, with a gleaming target on Natalie's back. He couldn't risk it.

"We'll have to stop for gas," he said.

"Car didn't come with a full tank?"

He shook his head. "Nothing here can be that easy."

"I guess not," she said softly.

Natalie had been silent since they'd started driving fifteen minutes ago, and Luke had let the silence stretch as he drove, processing what had happened back at the hotel. He would never know if he'd made the right choice in leaving Natalie in the room, but she was safe, at least.

For now.

A mix of fear and relief had been written all over her face when she'd opened the door for him earlier. He'd taken one look at her standing there—holding the jagged lamp stand, face pale, eyes glossy—and he'd been sure she was about to either cry or pass out. His first thought had been to get her to a chair, but somehow she'd wound up in his arms, and he'd been in no hurry to let go. He could tell himself all he wanted that he was just trying to offer comfort, but there had been something else there, too. He knew it, and he suspected Natalie knew it, as well. Because they had both lingered. Only for a few seconds, but a few seconds was enough to tell Luke he'd better not let it happen again.

The trouble was, Luke had spent so many years playing the role of brother-turned-single-dad, immersing himself in the lives of his two younger siblings, that he'd never had much time to date—until a handful of years ago when a young widow named Aimee came into his life. His sister, Triss, had been missing for weeks, her disappearance chalked up to teen angst by law enforcement. Aimee, familiar with loss, had stayed by his side and supported him in his endless search until Triss returned home one day, nearly ten months later.

His sister had never confided in him why she'd left, but he'd accepted her tearful apology and welcomed her home. From that point, his relationship with Aimee fizzled fast, as it became obvious that Aimee would never be able to fully accept Luke's commitment of responsibility to his siblings. But those few months with Aimee had sparked a longing that he had forced himself to put on the back burner for years: the longing for marriage, love, a secure home, kids of his own.

As much as he wanted that, he knew getting involved with Natalie would be a mistake. He knew, also from experience, that the client-agent relationship model was not one that usually ended well. Not to mention, she was still processing the canceled wedding and her missing ex-fiancé.

"Looks like something might be coming up," Natalie said, pulling him from his thoughts.

Luke let up on the gas as the shadowy outline of a large road sign began to take shape. "I think you're right." Gas and lodging at the next exit. They wouldn't stay there, but they could fill up their tank at least.

The road veered off sharply, and the car fishtailed for a split second before Luke got it back under control. Deliberately slowing down, he checked the rearview and peered down the adjacent street, on alert for any sign they'd been followed. All was quiet and dark. Too dark, with only a handful of dim parking lot lights.

Chances were slim that anything more would happen tonight, he knew that. But he prayed, anyway—a prayer he'd learned years ago at Vacation Bible School in his little Baltimore neighborhood in Cherry Hill.

Go before me and hedge me in from behind. Protect what I cannot. Exchange my doubt for faith and my fear for peace.

The prayer had seemed too simple to be powerful, but at twelve years old, Luke had been desperate. He'd clung to that prayer every morning and every night, his faith growing as he slowly learned to give his worries over to the One who could handle them all.

Time and God were faithful teachers, and the giving away grew easier with age, but as he pulled into the deserted gas station, Luke's hands clenched on the steering wheel, his chest tightening with tension he couldn't shake. There was no telling who was after them, or how they'd been tracked so well over the past twenty-four hours. He needed to fuel up and get back on the road before anyone had a chance to catch up with them. It was growing clearer by the minute that Natalie needed a security team—not a one-man show.

Pulling up to a pump, Luke took another glance around, assured that no one had followed them into the lot, and quickly got out, locking the doors behind him. The eaves of the gas station overhang didn't do much to keep the rain at bay, the wind forcing heavy drifts of rain against the car and Luke's back as he pumped gas and kept his eye on his surroundings. The numbers on the pump ticked slowly, and he was tempted to leave with just a few gallons—enough to get them to the hotel. He didn't dare risk it, though. Fueling up less now could mean another stop tomorrow, and the more they stayed out of sight, the better.

The glow of headlights caught his attention as an old black pickup truck slowly coasted down the adjacent road. He watched it, willing it past the station, but instead the vehicle slowed and turned into the lot. Luke glanced at his pump. Nearly twelve gallons. The small sedan probably didn't take much more than that, anyway. He hung up the pump, forgoing the receipt as he kept an eye on the truck pulling up to a nearby pump.

Natalie unlocked the doors for him and he quickly slid into his seat, water spraying off his jacket and dripping from his hair, his back wet against the seat. None of that mattered. What mattered was getting out of there fast. He started the car and pulled away from the station.

"The driver of that truck never got out," Natalie said, turning in her seat to watch the vehicle.

Luke had noticed. "We'll keep an eye out," he said. Hopefully, he was just waiting on the rain to let up. As Luke drove down the back road toward the highway again, he glanced in the rearview. The truck had stayed. No sign that they were being followed. He remained vigilant for several minutes until he was sure they hadn't been tracked down. Then he started to relax a little, focusing on the dark road ahead and the hope of a safer place to stay tonight.

He glanced at Natalie, half expecting she would be near sleep, but she sat upright, her profile lined with tension.

"Try to rest," Luke said. "He's not following us."

"I know he's not. But I somehow don't find myself tempted to curl up in my seat and take a nap at the moment."

Light sarcasm laced her words, and Luke grinned. "I guess not. Every time we start to relax, something else seems to happen."

"Exactly."

"The fire alarm was a bold move," Luke said thoughtfully. He'd been mulling over what had happened since they'd set out tonight. "The question is—was the guy waiting for you outside, or did he somehow know you were alone in the hotel room?"

"Or did he pull the alarm to get me out of the room so he could get inside without me there?"

"For what? Still looking for whatever he didn't find in your room earlier? Or finding a place to wait for you to return? I mean, once he unlocked the dead bolt, he knew you were inside. That didn't stop him."

"True. None of it makes sense."

"He wants you, or something you have. I want to circle back to Kyle for a minute."

"I really don't have anything to add. I kind of regret saying as much as I did, actually."

"Why? You're not the first person to stay in a relationship longer than you should have," Luke said, guessing as to why she felt so vulnerable right now. When she didn't argue, he continued. "But I'd be an idiot not to ask more questions about him. I asked Roman to see what he could find out about his financial situation, but there are limits as to what he can get his hands on."

"If you're asking me about Kyle's finances, I don't think there were any problems."

"The credit card issue is still a red flag in my mind."

"You think he was in some sort of financial trouble, and made the whole story up about the points?"

"It's possible."

"I really don't think so. He inherited nearly a quarter million less than two years ago from his grandfather. Money isn't something he had to worry about."

Two-hundred-and-fifty grand was a lot of money. Could the guy have blown through it all in two years? "He lives in a nice neighborhood. Those townhomes are pricey," Luke commented. "What kind of car does he drive?"

"He bought a Ford F-150 last year."

Luke knew Kyle's salary as a rookie public defender wouldn't go too far, considering where he lived—a prime spot in Federal Hill. "You mentioned he wanted a political career. Was he funding a campaign?"

"No. It was more of an in-the-future type of goal. But as far as I know, he had investments and didn't worry about money."

"But he wanted free airline tickets."

"He was frugal."

Luke felt like there might still be something there, but he sensed Natalie was done talking about her ex for now. Silence fell over the car as the rain let up, clearing his view of the dark road ahead. Luke let the silence stretch, mentally ticking off his plan of action for getting Natalie safely on that plane the next day.

By this time tomorrow, they would be on it. Twenty-four hours, and Natalie would be safely flying back to the States, and Luke would no longer be taking on sole responsibility for her protection. He just hoped that the past twenty-four hours weren't a predictor of what was to come.

FIVE

Lack of sleep was catching up with Natalie by the time she and Luke headed down the ramp toward the tarmac the next day. Long lines at the car rental return and then at security had delayed their expected departure by nearly two hours.

She glanced at Luke's profile. He didn't appear to be hurting for sleep, his dark eyes alert, his jaw clean-shaven.

She stifled a yawn, along with her frustration that they weren't already in the air. After all, today could have been a whole lot worse. They'd managed to check in to the new hotel last night, catch some sleep and get to the consulate's office right as it opened. Granted, that visit had stretched for hours, but they'd ultimately left with her passport in hand, so she wasn't about to complain.

Especially considering how relatively peaceful the day seemed so far. They'd spent no small amount of time looking over their shoulders and taking extra security measures, driving convoluted routes and keeping low profiles. But they hadn't seen one sign that they'd been followed to Cancun. Relief settled over her as they drew closer to the plane. No matter what was to come, she would be safer in the States.

Her gaze slid to Luke. He'd mentioned the community

center, and she wondered if he would be leaving Shield when they returned so he could continue to pursue that goal. Curiously, disappointment rose at the thought. She'd made a promise to herself that she wouldn't date again for a year, but she had to admit that she really liked Luke. He was the perfect cross between strong and protective, and easygoing and lighthearted. He was intense when he needed to be, but adapted based on the situation.

His hand settled lightly on her back as he kept his attention on their surroundings. It was a protective gesture she knew he'd been trained to do, but her pulse jumped around anyway, as if her fiancé had not ditched her at the altar two days ago, as if she hadn't been attacked, robbed and stalked on her solo honeymoon...as if some sort of meaningful connection had started to grow between them.

Whatever the reason for her dancing pulse, it evened out abruptly as they reached the steps to board the plane and Luke's hand fell away. The private jet stood sentry, door open to a long set of steps. Luke dropped back so she could go ahead of him.

Roman DeHart waited for them at the threshold, wearing a dark suit and a serious expression. He greeted them with handshakes and what could only be described as a grim smile.

"Make yourselves comfortable," Roman said. He gestured to the other agent on board. "Natalie, I believe you know Jordan Skehan."

Natalie waved to Jordan and sent him a smile she didn't feel. He and Kyle had been friends for years, but she'd always felt uneasy around him and couldn't put her finger on why. Roman hired him shortly after Kyle had introduced the two, and Jordan had been with Shield for just over a year. One of the younger agents on the team, he had bright red hair, a magnetic smile and light blue eyes that Natalie could never quite read. He nodded a silent and serious greeting, and Natalie moved farther into the cabin, suppressing the urge to question him about the morning of the wedding. Her questions could wait.

"Front row's outfitted with recliners," Roman said. "Grab a drink or snack if you want." He motioned to a fridge and a set of cabinets at the rear of the plane. "We'll be taking off in just a few minutes. Once we're in the air, we'll talk." He ducked into the cockpit.

Natalie sank down into a front-row seat at his suggestion, buckling herself in. Luke took the seat next to her, the narrow aisle between them.

It was time to go home. Her throat constricted and she closed her eyes to the emotions welling up. Relief. Sadness. Anger. Lingering fear. It was hard to believe how much her life had changed since Saturday morning.

Everything about her wedding day had been perfect—from the crisp morning breeze over the Chesapeake Bay right down to the vibrant purple mini calla lilies woven into white rose bouquets. An elegant water-view brunch reception had awaited inside Swan Cove Estates, and a trio of classical violinists had set the mood for romance as guests waited eagerly for the ceremony to begin.

When Kyle's text had come through, everything around her had faded. For one shattering moment, she had hoped he was playing a poorly chosen prank. Then she'd realized he was serious.

Her heart jolted. What had happened? She thought back to Friday night, reviewing the hours before they'd parted ways. By the time the rehearsal dinner had rolled around, they'd both been tired. Kyle had spent the last few nights pulling together a strategy for an impending case. Natalie had been tying up all the details of the big day while also juggling her regular clients along with a slew of new clients, plus her friend Julianna's busy public life, which was a job in and of itself.

Yes, they'd both been tired, but the night had been filled with a renewed sense of closeness that had been under repair since that red-flag night weeks before.

They'd sat close at dinner, then mingled with friends and family before exchanging their last kiss as an engaged couple. And then even though Kyle had said he wanted to get a good night's sleep, his friends had badgered him to go out with them on his last night as a bachelor. Had something happened that night? Or had he really just gotten cold feet? And if his cold feet excuse was true, then why the disappearing act?

These were questions she'd been mulling over for over two days now, but they had no easy or immediate answers.

"Ready to get home?" Luke asked.

She shrugged. "In a way. My schedule at work is packed, so it should help distract me." In fact, Julianna was organizing an extravagant Fourth of July charity fund-raiser for mental health services within the public school system, and Natalie was looking forward to getting a head start on the press releases. It was the best part of her job—publicizing worthwhile events that made a difference. She far preferred it to practicing interviews with clients who needed to spin stories and save their reputations.

"Really? You'll go back to work right away? I'd think you'd take a couple more days to recuperate."

"It's better for me if I stay busy. I just hope I can get my apartment back. My lease technically ends Saturday."

"Right. I guess you had already packed up and were ready to move."

She nodded.

"Are we taking you to your dad's place when we get back then?"

"No. I'd rather just go home."

"A boxed-up apartment sounds like a lonely place to go back to after a weekend like this one."

"I'm hardly ever alone. It might be good for me."

He looked like he was about to refute her, but Roman appeared again. He flipped down a seat attached to the wall across from Natalie, pulling on a seat belt as the plane rolled toward the runway. He had the darkest eyes she'd ever seen. She'd noticed it when she'd first met him a little more than five years ago, when her dad had switched to Shield from his previous security company. She'd also noticed his tailored suit, his dark gleaming hair, his professionalism and confidence. Though she had spent quite a bit of time at her dad's house during that time, she'd never thought of Roman outside the realm of family friend and her father's employee. His perpetual seriousness always unsettled her just a little, though that had changed slightly in the year since he'd gotten married.

"I've been in contact with a buddy of mine, Tyler Goodson. He's with the Baltimore PD. You need to know that there was blood found in Kyle's apartment."

Natalie's heart dropped. Here she'd been assuming he'd simply taken off, and there was blood…

"There's more," Roman said, the plane rolling fast along the runway, the engines loud. "He—or someone—emptied his savings account early Saturday morning."

A seeping cold filtered down her spine as the plane caught air and began its ascent. "How much was it?" she asked, her voice hollow.

"Police are keeping it under wraps," he responded, and she detected the slightest hesitation before he continued. "But they seem very interested in speaking with you about it. I wanted to give you a heads-up so you wouldn't be blindsided."

She appreciated his foresight, but the questions swirling in her mind were draining her energy.

Roman wasn't done, though. Turned out, he had barely begun. He pulled out a laptop and proceeded to grill her on every detail of her life—her work, her hobbies, her friends, her coworkers, her finances and, of course, her relationship with Kyle. The more knowledge his team had, he told her, the more effective they'd be at securing her safety. She got the impression that he planned to do some investigating on his own as well, though that wasn't part of his contract.

Eventually, just as Natalie was about to cry uncle, Luke chimed in. "Maybe some of this can wait," he suggested.

Roman glanced up from his laptop, his attention focused on Natalie. Whatever he saw must have been enough to convince him Luke was right. She was exhausted, and she probably looked it. Natalie self-consciously tucked a stray hair behind her ear and shifted in her seat. Roman closed his laptop and unbuckled his seat belt. "Looks like you're off the hook," he said, standing. He flashed an apologetic smile at her, a rare sight. It made him seem a lot less intimidating and a lot more human. "I'll let you get some rest before we land and you have to deal with everything back at home." He ducked out of the cabin and moved back to the cockpit with the pilot.

It was chilly in the cabin, and Natalie reached up to adjust the vent overhead. Then she pushed up her window shade, sunlight filtering in. She was aware of Luke's eyes on her, but she was steadfastly ignoring him, too aware of the quiet, the close quarters, the intimacy of the cabin with Roman gone and Jordan in the far back. Out of the corner of her eye, she saw Luke undo his seat belt and stand, then head toward the back of the plane. She closed her eyes, exhausted from answering all of Roman's questions, and not trusting herself to engage in conversation with Luke.

Every time their talks had veered away from her circumstances and into the realm of friendship, she found herself wanting to share more with him, and learn more about him. Meanwhile, as much as she wanted to fight the idea, it seemed like Kyle may not have disappeared willingly, which made Natalie's attraction to Luke all the more inexplicable. Plus, she'd vowed to steer clear of men for one year, and since she couldn't exactly get far away from Luke at the moment, her next best idea was to feign sleep.

She was certainly tired enough to fall asleep, anyway. The sun on her face warmed her, and she started to relax. Then a soft blanket settled over her, gentle hands tugging the edge up to her shoulders, Luke's nearness making her heart race, despite her silent pleas for it to relax. She expected him to move away, but he leaned over her, the fabric of his sleeve grazing Natalie's cheek. Her eyes flew open just as he started to slide the window shade back down.

"It's okay," she said, and he paused, his eyes meeting hers, the small space between them charged with what Natalie knew beyond a shadow of a doubt was mutual attraction. For one achingly brief moment, she thought he might try to kiss her. And that she might let him. His gaze dropped to her mouth, then moved back to her eyes, as if gauging her receptiveness. Or weighing the risks. He hesitated just long enough for Natalie to come to her senses. "I like the sunshine," she managed to say, purposely breaking the moment, even as her heart thrummed with longing. "But thank you."

"Sure," Luke said easily, and he left the shade alone

and straightened, quickly moving back to his own seat. Natalie was relieved. At least, that's what she tried to tell herself. Because relief made a lot more sense than disappointment. She shifted in her seat and watched out the window, wondering just what she would be going home to this evening, and whether she'd really be ready to face it all alone.

Across the narrow aisle, Natalie was quiet, her profile turned toward the clear blue beyond. Her hair was tussled in the back, and the soft blue blanket drooped away from her shoulders.

Luke's brother, Cal, had owned a blue blanket. Luke had salvaged it from a pile of someone's curbside eviction belongings. It had been worn and ratty, but it had been comforting. Luke had read somewhere that some kids felt more secure when they had something of their own to hold on to, like a blanket or a stuffed animal. Cal had carried that blanket everywhere.

He shook off the tender memory. It had seemed to come out of nowhere. But Natalie appeared young and alone as she looked out her window, and maybe a little lost, like Cal had often seemed—and sometimes still did.

Luke glanced out his own window at the speckles of thousands of houses miles below, the horizon that curved into a soft gray-blue until it disappeared around the earth, the puffy white clouds as the jet sliced through them.

"The view never gets old."

She looked his way. "You fly a lot?"

"A few times a year, for Shield."

She turned her attention back out the window. "Seeing the world from here always puts things in perspective."

"In what way?"

...minds me... I guess, just how small we—and our ...ms—are in the grand scheme of life."

...interesting perspective," Luke responded. "I look out the window and see the opposite. I see how big God is, how constant. We see specks for houses in one small corner of the earth. He sees every life, knows every name."

"I used to believe that," Natalie said, eyes solemn. "But if it's true...if He does see every life and know every name, why does He stand back?"

What he saw in her eyes was more than sorrow, worse than fear. It was doubt, and that was a path he'd walked down a time or two in his life.

"I don't think there's a person alive who hasn't struggled with that question," he responded. "I certainly have."

"And?" she pressed. "What do you do with it?"

He thought about that for a moment. "I have a wise friend who says that doubt builds when you stop feeding yourself truth. But sometimes, no matter how much I pray, no matter how much I read the Bible, I've just had to trudge through times of doubt until I could look back and see how God worked."

"Could you always see it?"

An image of the dark closet rose in his mind—confined, hot, rancid. And another of his mother, unconscious and heading to the hospital in an ambulance after another overdose, Cal and Triss grasping desperately to Luke as the CPS workers attempted to separate them. Deep emotion welled up that he hadn't allowed to surface for a long time. He cleared his throat. "I can't lie. I don't see His hand in every experience," he said. "But there's something I can always see when I look back."

"What?" Her eyes searched his for hope, for something to cling to.

"I can always see how He was there with me the whole

time. I don't think He stands back when we need Him, Natalie. He stands by and gives us strength to endure. And then, to overcome."

"Maybe," she responded softly, but she didn't look convinced.

Silent minutes passed and it wasn't long before Natalie had fallen asleep, the hours slipping by until the plane began its descent. She slept through the turbulence of the descent and the bounce of the landing, and only woke when Roman opened the cockpit door and asked how the flight had been.

"Wow. I really slept," Natalie said, sitting up and unbuckling.

"Good. You'll need your energy," Roman said. "A couple of things. First, the news has picked up your story. We'll do our best to manage the media, but you know how it goes."

Natalie nodded, looking unfazed.

Luke hadn't considered paparazzi, but then the media had always been interested in the Harper family. The judge's recent bid for governorship would definitely make Natalie's wedding-day disaster and subsequently missing fiancé a matter of public interest.

"Second, everything's fine, but your sister's been checked into the hospital with preterm labor, so—"

"She's still got four weeks until she's due," Natalie cut in, worry washing over her face. "Can you bring me there first?"

Roman nodded. "It's already been arranged." Then he passed a cell phone to her. "Picked up a replacement phone for you."

"Thank you."

Roman turned to Luke. "You good to stick around until third shift?"

"Sure." Luke wanted to see Natalie settled and safe before he headed home, anyway.

"You, too, Jordan?"

"I can do that."

Jordan had been so quiet, his eyes closed most of the flight, that Luke had almost forgotten he'd wanted to ask him about the morning of the wedding. As Roman ducked back into the cockpit while the plane taxied, Luke stood and made his way to the back of the craft to where Jordan was sitting. "Quick question for you."

Jordan looked up. "Shoot."

"Natalie said you and Kyle are buddies. You were a groomsman."

"Yeah. We've known each other for years."

"Did you see him the morning of the wedding?"

Jordan shook his head, a concerned frown on his face. "We were all meeting up at his cousin's place, and he texted us that he was running late. A while later, he texted that he'd meet us at the church. It wasn't like him."

"Any signs of distress the night before?"

Jordan shook his head again. "Nah. He was looking forward to the wedding. We had a good night out. I'm real worried about him."

The plane stopped and Luke thanked the guy for the information before turning back to lift the exit door, his mind working but failing to connect what little information he had into a story that made sense. What had happened between the time that Kyle had seen his parents and when he was texting his buddies? He was determined to do more digging once Natalie got settled, but for now, it was time to get to work watching her back again.

The media wasn't there waiting for them as they disembarked from the plane and crossed the lot to the airport. Cameras weren't waiting inside to snap photos. In fact, Roman's team had done such a professional job orchestrating Natalie's exit from the airport and transport to the waiting car, Luke was beginning to wonder if they'd managed to avoid publicity altogether.

Next to him, Natalie scrolled through her texts, replying to several and then listening to voice mails.

Finally, she flipped the phone facedown in her lap and stared out the window into the pitch dark of early morning.

Hunter was at the wheel, a Shield agent Luke had gotten to know and like over the past couple of years, and he and Roman were having a quiet conversation in the front. Meanwhile, Natalie had fallen silent.

"Looks like you have a lot of messages," Luke mentioned.

She nodded. "Mostly family and friends, with a few coworkers and reporters thrown in." She set her gaze out the window, but Luke didn't miss her tight grip on the phone, the tense set of her shoulders.

He tapped her hand. "If you're not careful, you'll crush your new phone by sheer might alone," he said lightly.

She relaxed her grip, and Luke pulled his hand away. Simple gestures that came naturally to him—gestures of protection, of comfort—felt more personal with Natalie. Every touch drew him closer to a line of professionalism he refused to cross again.

"I hope your coworkers were calling to check on you, not to give you a hard time about work."

"They were. For the most part."

"Well, work can wait a few more days."

"I'm actually looking forward to getting back. It's a busy time right now, and I'm up for partner."

"Wow, that's great." It didn't surprise him that she was

good at her job. Natalie seemed like the kind of person who didn't do anything halfway.

"Thanks. There are a couple people I work with who wouldn't agree. The argument is seniority versus profit generating."

"Some of the long-timers are a little jealous of your success?"

"You could say that. I brought on a new client last year—Julianna Montgomery."

Luke whistled. "The actress."

"Right. And once I started working with her… Well, she's big into networking, and so word of mouth…"

"And suddenly you had more than one extremely wealthy client?"

She nodded. "Honestly, it all kind of fell into my lap. So I get where some of my coworkers are coming from. But it's just the nature of the business."

They turned a corner into the hospital entrance, and Natalie sat up straighter. They hadn't escaped the media after all.

Ahead, news vans lined the lot. Cameramen and reporters crowded as close as they'd been allowed to get to the building, several police officers standing sentry to keep them at bay.

Next to Luke, Natalie observed the scene without comment. This was a scenario she was almost certainly used to, but maybe not in such a personal manner.

The scene turned Luke's stomach. He'd seen it time and again with clients whose cases found supporters and haters alike. Some reporters thrived on preying on people in pain. Tragedy and controversy made for the most compelling news after all. The idea sat festering as the SUV slowed and pulled to the curb near the hospital entrance.

The volume outside seemed to grow, pulsing around

the car, reporters closing in and shouting questions to Natalie, despite the closed and darkly tinted windows.

The driver shifted to Park, and Luke tapped Natalie's hand on the seat between them. "Ready?"

She nodded, her expression closed. Roman and Luke exited the vehicle in tandem, dozens of cameras flashing, reporters shouting questions, microphones thrust toward them, attempting to elicit a response from Natalie. But as he offered her a hand out of the SUV, she appeared calm. She was also silent, refusing to play their game. As she ducked her head to exit, her necklace swung out of the neckline of her shirt, and she palmed the ring, hastily tucking it back into her shirt before emerging from the vehicle with a single-minded focus on the entrance doors to the hospital.

Questions buzzed around them, and Luke was impressed with her serene expression, even as he noted her quickened pace.

"When did you last hear from Kyle?"

"Is it true he sent a text to call off the wedding?"

"Do you have a message for him if he's watching this?" They pushed through the crowd, and had almost reached the hospital entrance when a woman stepped in front of their path, a blue dress suit tightly hugging her figure, a shrewd expression on her face. She stuck a mic in Natalie's face and asked the first question that seemed to have any effect at all.

"Natalie, were you aware that your fiancé carried on affairs during your engagement?"

SIX

Natalie's heart stopped.

Everything stopped.

Affairs?

With each step, her composure slipped a little more. Luke pressed in close, urging her toward the sanctuary of the hospital. The doors opened ahead, tempting her to run. But she kept her stride steady, her head held high.

"Natalie!" the same reporter yelled. "Did you know?"

Against her better judgment, Natalie glanced back at the woman. Long shiny blond hair, a shapely body clothed in a business suit the color of the brightest summer sky. Only her questions and the cold expression on her face didn't make Natalie think of summer at all. Instead, as she turned away from the crowd and stepped into the hospital, she felt like she was entering the darkest, bleakest winter.

It wasn't until she'd stepped through the sliding glass doors of the hospital that she let her composure slip, felt the flush of humiliation warm on her cheeks. Could it be true? Could she have been so blind? She rejected the thought almost immediately. She worked closely with the media on a regular basis, and she had—in large part—a deep respect for the work they did. But she also knew that the nature of the job lent itself to nosing in on other people's private affairs and uncovering shocking information—true or speculative.

Well, they wouldn't be able to get anything from Natalie. She didn't plan to entertain them with a moment of her time. If Kyle had been having affairs, the truth would come out. Her ex's unfaithfulness had to take a back seat to someone far more important: Natalie's twin sister.

Clearing her focus, she was about to ask which floor her sister was on when she realized Luke was leading her on a mission. His arm rested on her back, his hand just below her shoulder blade, protecting and leading at the same time. He jabbed the elevator call button, and they walked inside together, Roman on her other side.

They rode up silently to the sixth floor, and Natalie was relieved neither asked her any questions. She was holding on to her emotions by sheer willpower, a willpower that was weakening by the minute. Her cell phone buzzed in her hand and she glanced down at it: her sister asking when she would arrive. She responded, trying not to think about the one person she had yet to hear from. When she'd gone through her phone she'd found messages from her sister, her stepmother, her dad, her two bridesmaids, Julianna and her boss. She had a few voice messages, as well. Two coworkers and a client. Julianna again. Two reporters.

But nothing from Kyle.

She didn't know what she'd expected. An explanation? An apology? Would either make her feel better? How could she have been so blind? Had their entire relationship been a lie? If he'd truly been having affairs, it would seem that way.

When the elevator doors slid back open, she forced herself to put aside thoughts of Kyle for the time being. Her sister needed her, and she suddenly couldn't get down the hall fast enough, practically bursting into Kristin's hospital room.

She rushed over to the bed, leaning down to hug her sister. "They told me you were okay, but I had to see for myself."

"Burst in here like that again, and you might throw me right back into labor," Kristin said with a laugh.

"Sorry." Natalie straightened and gave her stepmom a quick hug. They'd never been extremely close, but Stacy Harper was good for their dad and she'd always been kind toward the girls.

Stacy held on for an extra moment, which was unusual, but then pulled back and smiled. "I'm so glad you're home and safe. You really had us worried."

"I'm sorry. I should have—"

Stacy was already shaking her head, so Natalie stopped. "No apologies. I just wish you could have actually enjoyed that vacation. You certainly deserved it." She sighed. "Oh, you just missed your father. He saw one of Kristin's doctors in the hall and followed him. You know your dad."

Natalie laughed. "Yes, I do." Then she motioned to Luke at her side. "Have you met Luke Everett?"

"No, I don't believe we've worked with you in the past," Stacy said, extending a hand to Luke. "Pleasure to meet you."

"So you're the one who saved my sister," Kristin chimed in, smiling broadly, her hands splayed over her very pregnant stomach.

Luke grinned. "It was a team effort. You should see what she's capable of doing with a giant beach bag."

Kristin and Stacy both laughed.

"I can imagine," Kristin said, then focused her attention back on Natalie. "Good thing Roman was in contact with Luke. When I couldn't get ahold of you on your phone, I started to get really worried. Julianna and Hannah have been calling me hourly, too. What on earth happened to you?"

Natalie took the seat Luke offered to her, and then, in a detached sort of way, she relayed what had happened since she'd hopped on the plane out of Maryland on Saturday morning. Her sister and stepmother didn't interrupt, and she didn't stop until she had taken them all the way through her arrival at the hospital and the reporter's accusation about Kyle's affairs.

"I *knew* it!" Kristin said.

"You knew?" Natalie asked, incredulous.

"Of course, I didn't really *know*, or I would have told you. I just always pegged him as the type who wouldn't be happy with just one—" She stopped herself.

Natalie was glad. She didn't want to rehash the conversation she'd had with her sister and Stacy when she'd announced to them her engagement. Neither had been super excited about adding Kyle Paxton to the family. They'd told her she deserved better, more—someone who put her first, not his job and his connections.

The fact that her family hadn't loved Kyle should have sent her running, but it hadn't. Instead, she'd convinced herself that she understood Kyle more than her family did, and that once they spent more time with him, they'd like him more. She felt like a fool for that, but it was too late to go back. The weeks leading up to the wedding had flown by with family arriving from out of town, last-minute fittings and her sister's perpetual question every time they worked on wedding plans together.

Are you sure you want to marry this guy?

Some days, she hadn't been sure. But she'd pressed on. It was what she'd always done with commitments she'd made. And yet, she had nothing to show for it. Irony at its finest.

"I wonder if he ran off with one of those women," Stacy said, a frown on her face, but then shook her head. "But you said that there was blood…"

"How much blood are we talking?" Kristin asked, skeptical.

"I don't know. I'm hoping to get more information when I go down to the station."

Silence fell over the room as they all processed what may have happened. Natalie had a hard time believing something had happened to Kyle, but then the whole weekend had felt like a nightmare she kept hoping to wake up from.

"It's getting late," her stepmother finally said. "You and Kristin could both use some sleep. It goes without saying that we hope you'll stay with us, Natalie."

"I wouldn't mind staying here tonight, actually, keeping Kristin company…"

Kristin was already shaking her head. "I'll probably be heading home tomorrow. I'm fine—it was a false alarm. And you look exhausted."

She was right, and Natalie knew it. But she didn't want to go to her dad's. She just wanted to go back to her place for the night. She'd have to pull bedsheets from one of her boxes to put on the bed, grab a few groceries in the morning, but that was fine with her. For the first time in as long as she could remember, she actually wanted some time alone.

"I appreciate the offer," she said to Stacy, "but I think I'd rather just head back to my place."

At the look of disappointment on Stacy's face, Natalie almost backpedaled. It wouldn't hurt her to spend a couple days at her dad's house, and it would probably give him and Stacy extra peace of mind. But it was past time for Natalie to start standing up for what she knew she wanted. And she knew she wanted a little time alone to process all that had happened.

"I'm not in a hurry, though," she added. "I think I'll stay a bit longer."

"You look dead on your feet," Kristin pointed out. "I'm perfectly fine, and so is the bean."

Natalie laughed. Her sister had been calling this baby *the bean* for months, since she and her husband were at an impasse over names. "You don't have much time to come up with a name, you know."

Kristin sighed. "Maybe when I see her, I'll know what to call her."

"Let's hope so." Natalie stood up and stretched. "I think I'll run downstairs and get a coffee from Starbucks."

"You'll never sleep," Stacy chided.

"I'd need a lot more than a cup of coffee to keep me from sleeping when I get home later," Natalie said. "Do either of you want anything? Or something from the cafeteria?"

They both declined, and Luke opened the door to accompany her downstairs.

Jordan stood just outside the door, on duty. "Roman caught up with the judge in the cafeteria," he reported.

"That's where we're headed," Luke said. "Did Triss arrive yet?"

"There she is now."

Natalie turned to find a slender young woman walking toward them. Dressed in a black pantsuit, she wore her long straight hair in a sleek ponytail. She didn't look a day over seventeen.

"This is my sister, Triss," Luke said to Natalie.

The young woman held out a hand and clasped Natalie's in a strong grip. She didn't smile.

"Nice to meet you, Natalie."

"You, too. So you work for Shield, too?" Natalie asked, surprised at the family connection and even more surprised by how young Triss looked.

"Two years now."

"She's working while going to school," Luke added, a fatherly pride lighting his eyes. "Has her sights set on the FBI."

"Where are we headed?" Triss asked, clearly not interested in talking about herself.

"Downstairs for coffee," Luke answered. "You've got your assignment, right?"

Triss nodded. "Any news on the missing fiancé?" she asked him as if Natalie weren't walking right beside her.

"Not enough." Luke filled her in as they walked.

Bypassing the elevators, Triss opened the door to the stairwell. "Unless you're too tired, Ms. Harper, the stairs are probably the best way to go."

"I'm fine either way, but we did take the elevator up here," Natalie responded, confused.

"That was before I spotted a reporter hanging out by the elevators in the lobby." Triss headed down the first flight of stairs. "Besides, Luke hates elevators."

Did he?

Natalie met his eyes, but could read nothing in his expression. Not embarrassment or annoyance or even amusement.

They'd ridden an elevator back at the hotel in Mexico, hadn't they? The cement stairs echoed as they descended, the fluorescent light making Natalie's eyes ache. She refused to admit it to anyone, but she really needed sleep like Stacy had suggested.

Triss pushed open the door to the ground floor and let Luke and Natalie walk out ahead of her. Natalie knew where she was going, had been here the other three times her sister had gone into labor. She cut through the cafeteria, the scent of the cook-to-order grill only slightly cutting through the nauseating odor of sterile hospital rooms and hallways.

It was past dinner, but still busy.

"Looks like your dad's heading our way," Luke said.

Natalie looked up to see her father tossing wrappers into a trash can on his way toward them.

He smiled broadly, pulling Natalie into a bear hug and kissing her cheek. "You had us worried, Nat."

"Sorry, Dad."

"I'm just glad you're safe." Then his attention turned to Luke. Clasping his hand, he pulled Luke into a hard embrace. "You brought my daughter home safely. Thank you." Natalie's father stepped back, blue eyes bright with sincerity.

"My pleasure, sir," Luke said. "Have you been introduced to Triss yet?" He motioned to his sister.

"Earlier today. Nice to see you again, Ms. Everett," her dad said. "Where are you all headed?"

"Starbucks," Natalie said. "Want anything?"

"No, thanks. But since I've got you here, Luke, can we speak for a moment?"

Worry lines creased his forehead, and Natalie knew exactly what he wanted to speak with Luke about. He wanted Luke's take on what had gone down in Mexico—without Natalie there to temper his endless questions.

Luke turned to his sister. "You'll be okay on your own for a few?"

Natalie thought she caught a hint of an eye roll and the barest trace of a smile on Triss's face, but she couldn't be sure. "Yes," his sister said simply, and she and Natalie continued on their way as Luke followed Natalie's dad to an empty cafeteria table.

The Starbucks line was on the long side, and Triss stood practically shoulder to shoulder with Natalie as they waited. Natalie glanced over at the television monitors.

There she was on-screen, disheveled and tired, in shock. The cameras, the shouting reporters.

She couldn't hear the report over the din of conversation in the room, but she read the closed captions that described the canceled wedding, her hurried flight out of town, Kyle's disappearance and his ransacked apartment.

"Sources hint at secret affairs even as questions are raised about the ransacked apartment, Natalie Harper's quick wedding-day getaway and the engagement ring she's kept on a thin silver chain, hidden by her shirt."

The camera zoomed in on Natalie's hand as she captured the swinging necklace and hastily tucked it out of sight. Too late, of course. Her stomach dropped at a close-up still shot of the ring hanging from its silver chain.

Then the scene cut to a reporter just outside the police station as the Shield SUVs drove away. It was her again. The woman with all the questions.

A Channel 11 Twitter handle flashed at the lower part of the screen, and bright eyes under full makeup looked directly into the camera. "Natalie Harper, daughter of Judge William Harper, Republican candidate for governor, and stepdaughter of renowned pediatric neurosurgeon, Stacy Harper." The reporter paused, slightly raising her perfectly arched eyebrows. "Grieving bride-to-be? Or vengeful one? Tell us what you think."

A commercial came on and Natalie moved forward in the line, an odd numbness settling over her. She'd been through the whole gamut of emotions over the past two days, and she simply had nothing left at the moment.

"On second thought, I don't think I want coffee badly enough to wait in this line," she said, suddenly anxious to get out of line, out of the hospital, out of the middle of whatever it was she'd found herself embroiled in.

"You sure?" Triss asked, even as she hurriedly followed Natalie back through the cafeteria.

Out of the corner of her eye, she saw Triss nod at Luke, who was still sitting across the room with her father. "He'll meet us up there," Triss said.

She didn't tell Triss that she didn't plan to go back upstairs. She couldn't. Her chest felt tight, her mind reaching for a way out. The sliding doors opened into the long hallway, the elevators coming up on their right. But farther ahead was the hospital lobby—and the wide glass doors overlooking the parking lot.

Skirting past the elevators, she moved forward at a clipped pace toward the exit. She'd call her sister when she got back to her place. Kristin would understand, and Stacy would be glad she'd at least followed her advice to get some sleep.

"Ms. Harper, wait!" Triss's hand closed tightly over her wrist and Natalie yanked back, but the hand held fast. "Let me call up one of our vehicles," Triss said, slipping her cell phone out of her pocket.

"I'll take a cab. Please, let go." The words came out in a demanding tone Natalie didn't recognize as her own, but she didn't want to take them back. It was Triss's job to protect her, but she doubted the young woman would physically detain her against her will.

Sure enough, Triss dropped her hold, and Natalie ran out the door. "Let Luke know where I went!" she called, feeling guilty but determined.

Triss easily kept pace with her. "If I can't stop you, I'm going with you," she said as Natalie jogged up to the nearest cab.

The driver opened the door for them, and Natalie gave him her address as Triss pulled the door closed.

Luke's sister eyed Natalie, her expression unreadable. "So. Your apartment, right?"

"Yes."

"It would be wiser to wait until we have backup."

Natalie knew Triss was right, but she was acting on adrenaline and running on the reckless fuel of humiliation and anger. She shrugged, feigning indifference despite the tremor in her hands. "You're my backup. You seem fully capable."

Triss ignored the comment and started typing a message on her phone. Likely telling the whole crew where they were heading. She couldn't fault her for doing her job.

"I'm going to assume you're armed," Natalie said quietly so as not to alert the driver.

Without glancing her way, Triss reached down and pulled up the pant leg of her trousers, revealing an ankle holster. Then resumed typing.

"Excellent," Natalie murmured.

The elevator doors slid open and Luke breathed in the scent of Lysol and antiseptic with more relief than repulsion. He enjoyed elevators about as much as he'd enjoyed teaching his siblings how to drive. He and the judge had started up just a couple minutes after Natalie and Triss had left the room. He trusted his sister, but he found himself not quite ready to let Natalie out of his sight. He'd feel a lot better once they were back at the Harper estate with the security system he'd designed and installed—

and an entire Shield team at their disposal. Of course, Natalie didn't know about that plan yet.

It was the plan her father had wanted to discuss with Luke—after first thanking him for keeping Natalie safe and then handing him an envelope with a check for the full amount he'd been contracted for. Luke had pointed out that he'd only worked for the weekend, but the judge had cut him off, insisting on paying for the entire week and asking that Luke be part of the team moving forward until they were sure Natalie was safe.

It was an offer Luke wasn't going to turn down. He didn't need the money, but he felt compelled to stay on the team and see the job through to the end. Maybe she was already safe. Maybe getting her to the States was all he'd needed to do. But he had a bad feeling that whatever trouble had been chasing her in Mexico had followed her right back home, and he wasn't ready to step back from his responsibility for her safety.

He told himself it was because of his work ethic and his drive to finish every task he started, but he knew better. His desire to stay on the team was driven by the feelings he'd started to develop for the woman who had been a stranger just days ago.

His phone vibrated as they reached Kristin's room and Judge Harper tapped on her door. Luke froze, eyes lighting on the text on his phone.

On our way to Natalie's apartment in a cab. She refused to wait for anyone else. Backup?

His sister had sent it. She'd copied Roman and Jordan.

"Come on in," Kristin called from inside, and the judge walked in. Jordan looked up from reading the same text on his phone.

"I'll let the family know," Jordan said without hesitation.

"Thanks," Luke responded, turning and racing back down the hall. He started to call Triss, but a call from Roman was coming through. He picked it up.

"I'm getting the car now," Roman said. "I'll pull up to the front."

"On my way."

The elevator doors ahead were closing, and he ran toward them, jamming his foot in before they could close. The family inside jumped back and he apologized as he got on board with them, but he couldn't think much beyond anyone but Natalie.

What had she been thinking? She shouldn't have been taking a cab anywhere when they had a designated car with armed men at her service. And why hadn't Triss stopped her?

The elevator seemed to stop at every floor, letting people on and off, and Luke wondered if the stairs would have been faster. He was so focused on getting to Natalie that he barely registered the tight space, the doors trapping him inside again and again. Finally, they reached the lobby and Luke sprinted outside to where Roman was waiting with his dad, Carson DeHart, at the wheel. Cofounder of Shield, Carson had retired a couple years ago but missed the work, so he came back as a driver.

Luke jumped into the back, slamming the door shut even as Carson peeled away from the curb.

Roman turned in the front seat to face Luke. "I already let Triss know we're on our way. Fifteen minutes, tops."

Fifteen minutes wasn't a lot of time, but Luke knew that it was plenty of time for something bad to happen.

He texted his sister, suggesting she try to stall Natalie and keep her from entering the apartment until they arrived.

"She tell you she wanted to go back to her place?" Roman asked.

"She mentioned it, but we hadn't agreed on a plan yet."

"Did you talk to the judge?"

Luke nodded. "He told me the plan."

"You on board?"

"Absolutely."

"Good." Roman stayed facing Luke in the back. "What's your take?"

"On Natalie going back to her apartment? I couldn't say. On who's after her? I'll need help narrowing it down."

Roman looked surprised. "You dig up some enemies?"

Luke shook his head. "Not by any stretch." He filled Roman in on Natalie's theories about the kidnappings in Mexico.

"Possible," Roman said, but he didn't look sold.

"No doubt in my mind this has something to do with her ex."

"Agreed. I plan to do some more digging. I haven't been able to find anything on his finances yet, but our new intern thinks he can help."

"Haven't met him yet."

"Harrison Jenkins, just finished high school but the kid's a cyber-genius. Don't know if he can help us figure out who Kyle was involved with, but he can probably help with the financial side."

"Good." Luke tapped his finger restlessly on the seat next to him. "Carson, could you put it in high gear?"

"What else do you want me to do? Run the lights?" Carson asked sarcastically.

Luke rubbed the back of his neck. He'd sounded like a jerk, and he didn't know where that had come from. "Sorry."

He realized Roman was watching him silently.

"You okay, Everett?" Roman asked, his eyes observant.

"Fine. Jet leg's probably catching up with me."

"As long as it's just jet leg."

Luke waited for Roman to say more. They'd been friends for years, and Roman was always one for directness. But when Roman didn't add to the statement, Luke took the bait. "What are you trying to say, Roman?"

"Nothing you don't already know." Roman turned to face the highway again.

Luke could have let it go, but he was agitated, overtired and more worried by the minute about Triss and Natalie being off alone together with some madman on the loose.

"You're gonna have to spell it out for me."

Roman shrugged, not glancing back. "Just watch yourself," he said lightly. "This kind of trauma can be the worst foundation for a relationship. As you know."

Luke's immediate response was defense. "There's no relationship."

"Okay."

Roman's lack of argument was clearly not an agreement, and his nonchalance provoked Luke's irritation. "You and Ella seem to have a pretty solid foundation," he pointed out.

"Different scenario. We had history." He glanced back at Luke. "And I rest my case."

Luke balled his hand into a fist, frustrated, anxious,

irritated that Roman was calling him out like this. But he kept the thoughts to himself.

Roman was right about one thing. He needed to be careful. Growing up with a drug-addicted single mother who brought home an ever-revolving string of unpredictable men, Luke had learned at a young age that one-sided love was excruciating, and he promised himself it would never trap him again. Only it already had—twice. Aimee was the first woman he'd fallen hard for, a little over five years ago, a short-lived relationship built on the tenuous foundation of shared grief.

After Aimee, Luke had busied himself with work and planning his nonprofit for a couple years, and then he met Kendra, a Shield client. Kendra was fighting a court battle against her abusive and wealthy ex-husband, who was so determined to see her dead and incapable of collecting any of his money that he had hired an assassin to get rid of her. As the threats on her life increased, she and Luke became entangled in an emotionally charged relationship that had promptly ended when Kendra's husband was sentenced to prison and she went back to living her normal life, significantly wealthier.

Roman had pointed out then that Luke tended to fall for women who needed him, and the realization had taken Luke off guard. From that point on, though still longing for marriage, he determined not to let the pattern repeat itself a third time. Reluctantly, he had to admit that he'd be smart to keep that in mind. If Luke had learned one thing during his life, it was the delicate art of self-preservation.

Only, self-preservation didn't seem like a high priority right now. Not when Natalie Harper was minutes away from entering her unsecured apartment, weaponless and completely vulnerable. Oh, he knew that his sister was a tough adversary, but she was also young and somewhat green. And she'd have a difficult time defending herself and Natalie if they walked into a trap, especially if more than one person was lying in wait.

SEVEN

Ignoring all of Triss's arguments about why she should wait for the rest of the Shield team to arrive, Natalie stepped out of the cab and marched across her tiny patch of grass to the converted Charles Village row house she'd lived in and loved for the past three years. The two-story attached homes had been painted vibrant purples, blues and greens and repurposed as multiunit apartments. Natalie's was a one-bedroom with less than nine-hundred square feet, but she had made it home.

As she approached the door, though, apprehension suddenly took hold. Not because of Triss's unease, but because of the reality of what she'd face inside.

Boxes. All packed and ready to go to the new home she and Kyle had planned to share. She'd packed up most everything in the apartment before the trip. Kyle had even helped. The memory stuck there for a moment. By Wednesday of last week, she'd still had her entire office left to pack. Kyle had offered to help, but she hadn't wanted to burden him, so she'd declined.

She'd come home from work that night ready to pull an all-nighter, only to find the entire office packed up and a sweet card with a rose sitting on the desk. Kyle had borrowed her key and surprised her by taking care of the whole project for her, piling boxes high, wrapping up filing cabinets and desk drawers. The memory stung but also validated why she'd stayed in the relationship. He was forever doing things like that when she least expected it. She frowned. Come to think of it, he usually did those kinds of things after she mentioned he seemed distant or distracted.

She shook the thought away. She wouldn't waste time thinking about it.

As if she'd been there before, Triss led the way up the stairs and down the hall to Natalie's apartment. It didn't surprise Natalie. Roman would have thoroughly briefed his team on everything they would need to know.

She pulled out her key and reached for the knob, but Triss held out her hand.

"Let me take the lead."

Natalie set the key in her hand and dutifully stepped back as Triss first checked the knob. Locked, as it should be.

Triss unlocked the door and swung it inward, taking a quick sweep of the area before stepping inside, her arm out to prevent Natalie from going on ahead.

Natalie suppressed a sigh of impatience, watching as Triss smoothly retrieved her gun from her ankle holster. "Go ahead and lock up behind us," Triss said.

Natalie turned the bolt.

"You have an alarm, right?" Triss flicked on the living room light and edged farther into the apartment.

"Yes."

"Was it set when you left?" Triss stepped down into the recessed office. Not much to investigate there, but the woman was thorough.

"I don't really use it. Plus, my neighbor, Gretchen, was taking care of my cat," Natalie explained, following Triss. "She didn't want to fuss with the alarm."

Triss said nothing as she stepped out of the office and did a walk-through of the kitchen, flipping open cabinets and peeking into the pantry. Natalie followed at her heels, waiting for the go-ahead. At the edge of the kitchen, a short hallway led to the bathroom and bedroom. It was dark, both doors closed. She'd left them that way so Taser would have fewer places to hide from Gretchen. Speaking of Taser…

Natalie glanced around. Usually, her cat greeted her when she came home. Maybe he was in hiding since she'd been gone a few days.

Triss started down the hall, but held up a hand to stop Natalie. "Wait here until I check it out."

Suppressing impatience, Natalie dutifully retreated back into the living room, standing by the plastic-wrapped couch.

Boxes lined the walls, waiting for the movers to come in a few days. She'd need to cancel, assuming her landlord would let her renew the lease. The thought didn't upset her. She'd always felt at home in this little place, with its original brickwork and carved mantel fireplace, its hand-scraped wood floors that had seen over a hundred years of living.

Down the short hallway, Triss entered the bathroom, flipped on the light and spent a few seconds inside. Then she turned back into the hall and opened the door to the bedroom. A loud thud sounded from the room, and Natalie jumped, edging toward the sound.

"Triss?" she called, rushing toward the bedroom door.

"I'm fine," Triss said. "It was just your cat."

Taser tore out of the bedroom, skidding across the sleek wood floor as if fleeing sure death. Heart in her throat, Natalie laughed at her own jumpiness and crouched down to pet him. He was a six-month-old spitfire, and Natalie loved him, with his charcoal gray coat and white-tipped tail.

"Did you miss me, little guy?" She scratched him behind the ear as he purred. How had he wound up trapped in there? "What were you doing in my room, any—"

A sharp yelp came from her bedroom.

Natalie shot to her feet as a loud crash sounded.

"Triss? Are you okay?" She ran down the hall and into the bedroom. She'd piled furniture and boxes too high in her room. Now they were spread across the floor, two on top of Triss, their contents spilling out.

"Triss!" She knelt beside her next to the bed near the adjoining bathroom, shoved a couple of heavy boxes away. Triss's gun lay by her right foot. There was blood on the floor, pooling under her left side.

A lot of blood.

Too much for a fall. And Natalie would have heard the gun if it had accidentally gone off. Had she knocked into something? Broken glass and fallen on top of it?

"Triss?" She felt for a pulse, relieved at the slow, steady beat she found.

"Stand up," a man growled behind her, and Natalie screamed, jumping back from Triss and pivoting around.

A nylon mask covered his face, his features distorted and terrifying. Almost as terrifying as the blood-covered knife in his hand.

He moved away from her closet and blocked the bedroom doorway. Her only way of escape.

Natalie screamed again, backing up hard against her nightstand. Her attention darted to Triss's gun on the floor.

"Don't!" the intruder roared, and he lunged at her. Natalie scrambled up onto the bed in a desperate move to evade him.

He followed her, catching her hair in his hands as she jumped off the bed again. Her head yanked backward, the knife flashing by her face as he slid off the bed behind her. Tears sprang from her eyes at the ruthless grip of the man's hand on her hair. It was the man from the beach. She knew it. Knew it from his forceful grip, his smoky odor, the bulk of his body yanking her back against him.

She spun away from his grip with momentum, her rusty self-defense training kicking in as she slammed her hand into his chin with enough force to send him reeling back.

Go, go, go! her mind screamed, and she was trying, sliding across the wood floor, bursting into the hallway, her sights on the front door.

He tackled her from behind, and she went down hard, her knees smacking first, then the side of her face.

Natalie rolled to the side before he could pin her to the ground, kicking back hard. Her heel connected with hard bone, and the intruder grunted, but his gloved hand caught her hair again, whipping her neck back and throwing her onto her back.

Just when she thought she was trapped, she remembered something else she'd learned years ago. Gathering her strength, she jabbed his throat with the side of her hand.

The man made a strangled sound, a hand coming to his throat. It was just a split second, but she used it. Twisting out from under him, she jumped up and flew down the hall, screaming for help. The front door was just feet away.

It registered then that someone was pounding on it. Sirens wailed, just blocks away.

"Natalie!" Luke's voice sounded from the hallway. The

door shook violently under the pounding. "I'm breaking this door down!"

Natalie reached out for the dead bolt, but Luke slammed against the door again and she reared back as the frame cracked, but the door held.

She swung a glance over her shoulder, feeling blindly for the lock. The intruder hadn't followed her. Natalie fumbled with the dead bolt and the door flew open as she unlocked it, Luke and Roman bursting in.

"Some guy just dropped off the porch roof and took off," came a voice on Roman's radio. "Turning around to try to follow."

"Are there others?" Luke asked.

"I only saw one."

Luke and Roman exchanged looks.

"I'm on it," Roman said, and ran out the door.

"Are you okay?" Luke asked, settling his hands on her shoulders, his eyes skimming her for any signs of injury. "Where's Triss?"

"She's hurt." She ran back to her room, Luke following, and sank down on the floor next to Triss. Luke crouched over his sister, pulling back her jacket to reveal the growing bloodstain on her side. The sirens outside drew closer.

"We need to stop the bleeding," he muttered, yanking off his jacket and pressing it against his sister's side.

Triss moaned, her eyes opening. "Where'd he go?" she asked, struggling to sit up.

Luke pressed his free hand against her shoulder, holding her down. "Nowhere you can follow. You're getting an ambulance ride."

"He was hiding behind the boxes." Her words were slurred, her eyes half closed.

"He hit you with something?" Luke asked, his voice

gruff, hand gentle as he pulled aside her dark hair and eyed a reddening bruise near her eye.

"I don't know. He came around the boxes and got me with a knife." She closed her eyes, and Luke frowned.

"Try to stay awake," Luke urged his sister, and Natalie's heart ached with the sight of the tears in his eyes, the pallor of Triss's skin, the blood poured out on the floor.

Triss's eyes fluttered open, just barely. "I'll be okay," she whispered, letting her eyes drift shut again. Natalie wasn't sure she was right. Even the trample of paramedics and police charging up the stairs didn't reassure her. The hospital was nearly ten minutes away and Triss was still bleeding, bright red seeping straight through Luke's jacket and into his hand.

It had been years since Natalie had really prayed about anything, but desperation turned the clock back nearly two decades, to the day her brother had gone missing, and suddenly her eyes were closing, her hand slipping over Triss's shoulder, and she was pleading silently with God to save Triss's life.

She knew better. She'd prayed when Liam had gone missing, but he'd still been murdered. And she'd prayed when depression had latched onto her mother and strangled her will to live, but her mother had still died. Still, it was the only thing she knew to do, the only hope she had to cling to. Because if Luke's sister died, Natalie would never forgive herself.

Seventeen minutes in, and hours to go. Luke shifted in his chair and scanned the nearly empty waiting room. Triss had lost a lot of blood. Nearly three pints to be exact. The nine-inch blade had found its way straight to her right kidney, and the injury was serious. If she died…

No. He wouldn't let himself go there. She was a fighter. She would live.

But doubt crept in and assaulted him with memories. Newborn Triss, shaking and wailing in what he later learned were the cruel effects of cocaine withdrawal. The frail baby who never cried for food because she learned crying never got her what she needed, anyway. Luke had figured it out himself before he'd turned eleven. He'd read up on baby care, and he'd set alarms for himself during the day and at night to remember to feed her, since their mother couldn't be counted on.

Toddler Triss, sweating, near death, left in the car when Luke had come home from school the last Friday they'd spent as a family of four. Triss, the kindergarten spitfire, knocking down girls *and boys* on the playground. The quiet preteen silently enduring unspeakable abuse at the hands of foster parents. The teen runaway, and her return. She couldn't die now. Not when she'd overcome so much. Not when she was finally making headway in the world. Going to school, going to work, setting goals and achieving them. Even smiling from time to time.

He rubbed his hands over his face, fighting the unfamiliar sting of tears. Crying had never done him any good. But for once in his life, he could do without the responsibility of the world on his shoulders. He'd gotten a taste of what that felt like a few years ago when Aimee had entered his life. Maybe he'd been lonely for too long to know the difference between love and codependency, or maybe he just hadn't realized how much he longed for companionship, but there was something about having someone around to bounce ideas off of, to share grief and worries with, to pray with, that introduced him to what he'd been missing. It wasn't something he spent a lot of time fixating on, but it was times like this—sitting alone in a hospital waiting room, hoping to hear that his sister was going to survive—when he remembered what he didn't have.

Footsteps and quiet voices from down the hall drew his attention, his pulse racing as he half expected a doctor to round the corner. Too soon for good news, which could only mean one thing...

But it wasn't a doctor who rounded the corner. It was Roman—with Natalie.

"How's she doing?"

Roman was asking the question, but Luke's attention was on Natalie. She appeared relaxed in white jeans and a blue hoodie, but Luke's response to her was anything but relaxed, his rapid-fire pulse surprising him.

"Surgery started about twenty minutes ago," Luke answered. "I thought you'd be at your dad's by now."

"We thought you could use some company." Natalie handed him a bottle of water and took a seat next to him.

Roman stayed by the entrance, leaning against the door frame. "She had to get her shoulder stitched back up. ER took a long time."

"I didn't realize you'd been hurt," Luke said.

"I didn't, either. Roman noticed the blood before I did."

"And I told her she probably needed sleep more than you needed company, but she didn't agree." If Luke knew Roman at all, he knew exactly what he'd been thinking: the safest place for Natalie was back at her dad's house. But Shield's purpose was to protect their clients during their everyday life. Roman would have pointed out his concerns, but he wouldn't interfere with personal decisions. He would simply set up security to the best of his ability to mitigate the risks.

Luke turned back at Natalie, caught off guard by a

swell of emotion that somehow crossed the barrier of gratefulness and moved right into a deep sense that Natalie understood him.

"You've been through enough. You don't need to stay here. It could be hours."

She looked at him seriously, her expression unreadable. "Do you want me to leave?"

"I just don't want you to feel obligated."

"I don't."

Luke felt Roman's eyes on them, and he glanced up to find him turning from the room. "Jordan's just in the hall here," he said. "I'll check in with the rest of the team and be back in a few."

Seconds passed silently after Roman left, and then Natalie spoke up. "I'm sorry. I should never have left the hospital tonight."

"Triss shouldn't have, either, and I shouldn't have let either of you walk out of that cafeteria." He ran a hand down his jaw and sighed.

"You and your sister seem close."

"I pretty much raised her. My brother, Cal, too."

"What about your parents?"

"Dad was never in the picture," he said. "Mom was an addict. Disappeared for days at a time. She was in and out of rehab, winning us back in the courts and then losing us again."

"So you took on the role of parent?"

"Something like that. I got books from the library, read about babies and figured out Triss needed a nap and feeding schedule. I found an old broken stroller waiting for the dump and rigged it up so we could go on walks. Even got a bedtime routine going."

"Mr. Mom."

"That was me. In some ways, I liked it. But it was a

lot of pressure. And the worst part was we were always hungry."

"I can't imagine," Natalie murmured.

"At some point in middle school I realized that Mom probably wouldn't be around much longer," he continued. "I knew the system by then. We'd already been split up a few times, sent to different foster homes. I worked really hard, graduated high school two years early, worked my way through college by the time I was nineteen. So I could fight for custody of my siblings if I had to."

"And you had to?"

He nodded. "Mom died two days before I graduated."

He saw the sympathy in Natalie's eyes, was about to assure her that he'd managed okay, but her hand settled on his arm. "I'm so sorry." Everything good and comforting and warm was in that simple touch, in the soft expression in her eyes. Her sincerity took his breath away. All his life, he'd taken care of other people, and he liked it that way. Only, he craved more. He longed for someone to share life and burdens with.

He pushed his thoughts aside. They were pointless, fruitless thoughts, anyway. Clients were off-limits, especially emotionally vulnerable clients in turmoil. "We all struggle," he reasoned. "If we didn't, we wouldn't grow." That was a hard-won truth. Another truth was that there were days when he didn't want to struggle alone. Where he thought about things like family and children and going home to someone who was as anxious to see him as he was to see her. So far in life, every time he'd risked loving, he'd ended up losing. He was logical enough to realize that staying single was not the answer, but also practical enough to be cautious about jumping into a relationship.

When Natalie didn't immediately respond, Luke

changed the subject. "Any word on the intruder? I feel out of the loop."

"I think Roman just wants you to be able to concentrate on your sister," Natalie said. "But there's not much to report. The police are canvassing for an abandoned car nearby, checking cameras on the street."

"Did you get a good look at him?"

She shook her head. "But I'm almost positive it was the guy from the beach. Not sure how he could have followed us, though."

Luke shrugged. "Anyone could guess you'd stop by your place sooner rather than later. Or maybe he didn't know. Maybe he was looking for something and you caught him by surprise."

Natalie shuddered. "Triss's gun was right there on the floor," she pointed out. "He could have grabbed it when I ran out of the room. Why didn't he?"

Luke shook his head, just as puzzled as she was. "We'll have to go back later. Take a look around and see if anything's missing. Roman's activating the security system and putting a few guys over there."

"He told me about the plan to stay at my dad's for a few days. I'll need to pick up my cat. Thank goodness Gretchen didn't walk in on the guy."

"The team can take care of the cat until you move back in."

She didn't look convinced, but she didn't argue. "What did the doctor say about Triss?"

"They're going to try to save the kidney. She's lost a lot of blood." An ache rose in his throat, sharp and unexpected. He cleared it away.

Natalie set her hand on his arm again, tenderness and compassion in her touch. "I've only spent a few minutes with your sister, but it was enough time to tell me she's a strong woman. That's supposed to be half the battle in a medical crisis, right? The will to live?"

Luke couldn't help but smile at that. "She's always been a fighter."

Natalie returned the smile and started to draw her hand away, but Luke covered it with his own, keeping her there a moment longer.

"Thanks for coming back tonight." She couldn't possibly know how much the gesture meant to him. "I'm sure the hospital is the last place you want to be right now."

A spark of humor shone in her eyes. "Well, I don't know. My other option was to settle in for the night at my dad's—and he has a lot of questions for me." She tugged her hand out from under his, grabbed a magazine from the coffee table and started flipping through it.

Luke saw right through the act, knew she was rejecting the inexplicable connection that kept sizzling between them. He also knew it was for the best. "So. By process of elimination…"

"Hospital won out," she filled in, flashing a grin up at him and then turning her attention back to the magazine.

That was fine. She could spend the rest of the evening silently reading a magazine next to him, and Luke would be content. Something about Natalie's presence felt right and solid and like everything he'd been missing out on for years. It wouldn't last. It couldn't. But he'd hold on to that feeling while he had it.

A whirring hum sounded from around the corner, and Luke watched the entryway, surprised when a double-wide stroller came into view, Hunter Knox at the helm with Roman's wife, Ella, by his side.

Luke jumped up, surprised. "What are you two doing here?"

"Keeping you company." Hunter walked around the stroller, clasping Luke in a quick hug. "How's she doing?"

"Haven't heard anything for a while. Still in surgery." Luke's attention strayed back to the stroller, where Roman's very pregnant wife was tucking a blanket more securely over Hunter's two sleeping toddlers.

"It's past ten—you didn't have to come. And bringing the kids out and everything…"

Hunter grinned. "My kids just about kill me with their energy, but they make up for it in sleep. They didn't make a peep from their beds, to the car, to the stroller."

"I haven't been sleeping much lately, anyway," Ella added as she straightened and then hugged Luke awkwardly, her swollen belly getting in the way. "Roman said Hunter would let me tag along." Her attention shifted toward Natalie, and she turned, beelining across the room to introduce herself, taking the seat that had until moments ago been Luke's.

More voices began filtering down the hall, and Luke fought back rising emotion as more friends and coworkers began to fill the once-empty space, talking quietly, offering encouragement, just sitting together waiting.

When had he last felt like this? So supported? So cared about? Had he *ever* felt like this? He couldn't bring up one memory. And then Roman reappeared, surveying the scene with a nod.

"Looks like everyone's here," he said, crossing the room to his wife and holding out a hand to her.

She smiled and stood, folding her hand into his and leaning close, her gaze searching out the faces of the friends who had shown up. "I thought we could all pray together," she suggested. "Maybe just all circle around?"

Ella held out a hand to Natalie, and Luke's heart swelled when she took it to join the quickly forming circle. He got the sense that she didn't pray much, but she was willing to step out of her comfort zone for his sister, for him.

The circle widened, hands linking, and Natalie met his eyes, holding her other hand out to him. He grasped it tightly, the smooth warmth of her skin a balm to his worry as new hope rose—not just for his sister, but also for lasting friendships that would help carry him no matter what the future held.

EIGHT

Luke scooted his chair closer to Triss's hospital bed, tenderly rubbing the top of her hand where it lay at her side. Natalie's throat tightened at the gesture and their obviously close sibling bond. Triss had come through the surgery and would recover, but it would take several days before she felt 100 percent.

"It seems like it's taking a long time for her to wake up," Luke said, his face drawn with worry.

"I'm awake," Triss muttered, "but opening my eyes makes me want to puke." She opened them, anyway.

"Keep them closed then," Luke said, squeezing her hand.

She stared up at him seriously. "I'm really sorry, Luke, I—"

"Don't apologize. You should never have been on your own."

"Not about that," Triss said, and the barest hint of a smile tugged her mouth up. "I spy another gray hair."

Luke laughed, the sound rich and contagious, and Natalie found herself grinning, too. Who knew that Triss had a sense of humor somewhere under all that bravado?

"You're responsible for every single one," Luke agreed.

"You made it out okay," Triss said, her attention moving to Natalie.

She nodded. "I'm sorry, Triss," she said, her voice gritty. "I never should have pressured you to let me leave the hospital. I don't know what came over me."

Triss waved a hand, dismissing the apology. "We both made mistakes—you shouldn't have run off without waiting for backup. And I should have kept you from leaving, even if that meant tackling you to the ground. Which I *will* do next time."

The image brought a grin to Natalie's face. "There won't be a next time. I plan to follow the rules from here on out."

"Good." Triss turned her attention back to Luke. "It happened so fast. I didn't even know it was a knife. Felt like I'd been punched. Next thing I know, I'm falling into boxes. That's all I remember."

As Luke filled his sister in on the rest of the story, Natalie relived the moments in her apartment, images flashing in her memory—distorted features under a nylon mask, Triss on the floor, the gun. Blood, its tinny odor filling her nostrils as it seeped onto the wood floor, dripping into the seams.

Luke's cell phone buzzed and he checked it. "Roman will be here in five minutes." He stood. "I'll walk Natalie down and get her in the car, then come back up."

"Go home, Luke," Triss said.

"I'm staying with you."

"I'm a big girl," his sister chided. "I can take care of myself."

"I'm not leav—"

"The last thing I need is for you to sit here hovering over me while I sleep tonight."

Luke hesitated and Triss looked back at him, her gaze unwavering. "Anyway, you need a good night's sleep as much as I do, and you could use a shower, too. If you know what I mean."

"That was kind of low," Luke said with good humor.

"You've always insisted on total honesty," Triss replied with a teasing shimmer in her eyes.

It was obviously a ploy to get Luke to leave. Natalie was standing right next to him, her face just inches from his shoulder. A trace of his cologne remained, conjuring images of moonlit forest paths and romance.

She edged back. *Romance? If anyone needs sleep, it's me.*

"I know how to take a hint." Luke bent to drop a kiss on her forehead. "I'll be by first thing in the morning. Call me if you need anything."

Luke looked as tired as Natalie felt, and almost as defeated, as they walked side by side toward the elevators. She reached out to press the call button, but at the last minute remembered his aversion to elevators.

"Let's take the stairs," she suggested, bypassing the bank of elevators and heading across the hallway.

Luke pushed the stairwell door open and they started the nine-story descent, their sneakers padding unhurriedly along the concrete steps. He was uncharacteristically silent, and Natalie stole a glance at him, noting the obvious anxiety in his expression.

"Your sister's one tough cookie," she remarked, hoping to encourage him.

"She always has been. Tonight, though… Well, there were a lot of people praying for her."

There certainly had been, and Natalie wouldn't deny that there was something bonding about a group of friends and believers gathering in prayer like they had tonight. Natalie had never been a part of something like that. Prayer had always been more of a token comfort for her than a faith tool.

"Prayer or no prayer, she's a strong girl," she pointed out. "People pray for a lot of things they don't get."

"True," Luke said. "I prayed for years that my mom would get clean, get better. She never did. But I prayed other prayers over the years that He distinctly answered."

"Some would call that chance. Not answered prayer. Why answer one prayer and not another?"

"I'll never know why God didn't lift my mom out of her addictions and make our family a safe place, but I always knew He was there, carrying me to where I am today."

In her heart, Natalie knew he was right. No one was promised a life without heartache, but only that they wouldn't walk through it alone. Still, it was a tough pill to swallow after losing two of the people she had loved the most.

An SUV was waiting at the curb in front of the hospital entrance. An older gentleman came around the side of the vehicle and waved at her, opening the back door. "Hello, young lady," he said.

"Hi." She paused before getting in the car. His eyes looked familiar. "Have we met before?"

"Haven't had the pleasure." He extended a hand and shook hers warmly. "Carson DeHart, at your service."

Recognition sparked. The eyes. He looked just like Roman. "You're Roman's father?"

He nodded proudly, his eyes kind. She remembered then the story she'd heard about Roman's sister. Brooklyn's murder had been tragic, and Natalie knew firsthand the trauma and grief that rose from a situation like that.

"They keep trying to get me to retire, but they can't fire the cofounder."

She laughed and climbed into the SUV, her heart already flipping at the sight of Luke waiting for her.

As Carson pulled away from the hospital, Roman acknowledged them both and returned to a conversation he was having with his dad about a new potential client. Meanwhile, Natalie couldn't stop thinking about Luke's words.

She felt strangely close to him, as if she could talk to him about anything, and she found herself curious about something he had said.

"What you said back there…about never being alone?" she asked quietly. "When did you start to really believe that?"

He looked over at her, the dark interior of the car hiding his expression. "Oh, I was about ten, I think. Triss was a baby, screaming. It was nap time and she was hungry. There was nothing in the apartment. Mom had been gone longer than usual. Three or four days. I was desperate. My brother, Cal, was four at the time and I told him I needed to go get us some food. He was screaming, 'Don't leave me! Don't leave me!' I didn't know what to do. I'd planned to steal something from the shop on the corner. I couldn't do that very easily with a screaming baby and a four-year-old with me. So I closed myself in the bathroom and started crying, too."

The image of him as a little boy, desperate, alone, hungry, tore at her heart.

"This is where it gets good," he said with a light in his eyes. "I prayed right then. I said, 'God, if You're real, You can give us food. I can open the fridge, and something will be there.' And I begged and pleaded and ran to the kitchen, opened the fridge."

He looked at her, eyes shining with the memory. She almost expected him to say food had miraculously appeared in a cupboard he'd overlooked.

"Nothing," he said. "Every part of me wanted to run

out then and never come back, never have to hear my hungry baby sister cry again or worry about CPS finding out that we were without a parent again. Triss cried for hours before she fell asleep. Cal had fallen asleep, too. I was thinking about leaving them to run to the store, but I was worried. They were so little to be left alone. Then there was a knock at the door."

Natalie was there with him, sitting in his little kitchen, all the open cabinets bare, his young siblings passed out from tears and hunger.

"It was a neighbor. She had two big brown paper bags full of groceries. Said she thought we might be needing some things."

Gooseflesh broke out along Natalie's arms and she rubbed it away. "What'd she bring?"

"Honey Nut Cheerios, milk, graham crackers, bread, peanut butter, bananas. I remember everything I took out of those bags. I'll never forget it."

"That's pretty incredible."

His story intrigued her. She wanted to know more about this man who had sacrificed his childhood, who had put his dreams on hold, to raise his siblings. This man who had the kind of faith that somehow tugged at her soul, touching on questions and hopes she'd stuffed down for more than half of her life. If the timing were different, if their circumstances were different...

She shut the thought down immediately. The timing was wrong. The circumstances could not be worse. And she'd made a promise to herself.

Luke let the memory fade away again. He hadn't thought about it in a long time, but it had been a defining moment in his life—one that he would never forget.

"You know what I complained about to my sister a

couple weeks ago?" Natalie asked after a long silence. Her voice was soft, tired. "I told her my life had always been predictable." She sent a resigned grimace his way. "I think I like predictable."

"There's nothing wrong with that. Predictability creates a sense of security."

She nodded. "For the first time in my life, I have no idea what's coming."

"Do we ever really know what's coming?"

She was quiet for a moment. "Maybe not. I guess somewhere along the way I started to think I was in charge."

"In charge of decisions, maybe. Outcomes, not so much." Luke could use the reminder himself. How long had he done everything on his own? He was still reeling from the gathering earlier at the hospital, and the outpouring of support his friends and coworkers had brought, despite the inconvenience. Even Hunter with his two little kids and Ella with her pregnant belly. Truth was, he was tired of going it alone all the time. Tired of buying into the belief that everything was on his shoulders.

"It's unsettling."

"A little," Luke agreed. "But, in a way, maybe it's freeing, too."

She stared back at him, her expression unreadable in the dark shadows. "I don't know if I'd go that far."

"I just think if we can get to a place where our hope is in God and not ourselves, there's a certain amount of peace that comes from that."

"It sounds so simple."

"It is, I guess," Luke replied.

She said nothing as the vehicle turned onto Luke's street. He hadn't realized the plan was to drop him off.

Carson pulled up in front of his redbrick Canton townhome.

"I don't mind finishing out the shift," he said.

Roman turned toward him. "You'll do us more good when you're rested up."

He couldn't argue with that, even if he wanted to, so he opened the door and climbed out. "Have a good night and stay safe," he said to Natalie.

"Good night, Luke." She gave a small wave, and he shut the door, heading up the dark walkway to his house.

It was a humid night, but still cool, the sounds of frogs and crickets and other night creatures echoing from the nature preserve behind his house. He'd always liked the sound, and slept with the windows open whenever the weather let him get away with it. Tonight, though, the echoes felt lonely somehow. He almost would have rather stayed at the hospital with Triss, but he recognized her look of mutiny when he saw it, and knew if he stayed, she'd just badger him all night until he left. It was probably for the best, anyway. He didn't like to admit it even to himself, but fatigue was quickly catching up with him.

He unlocked the front door and flipped on the foyer light, stepping out of his shoes and crossing through the living room to the hallway to head toward his bedroom. The house was silent without Triss there. Cal had been gone for a couple of years, had just finished his second year with the army, but Triss had opted to stay with Luke and save money while finishing her forensic science degree. He wasn't in a hurry for her to go. He imagined this must be what it felt like to be an empty nester. Except he wasn't a father and he didn't have anyone to share the empty nest with.

His thoughts turned to Natalie, but just as quickly turned away. He'd do himself a favor and pour all his energy and resources into getting his nonprofit off the ground. He wouldn't let that plan get derailed again. He

reached into his pocket and slipped out the envelope that
Judge Harper had given him. He'd deposit the check tomorrow and go online to pay Triss's fall tuition. Then
he'd head over to his building and see how the renovations were coming.

After a quick shower, he picked up his phone to set
his alarm for the morning and realized he'd missed a
text from Natalie.

Just FYI—realized my ring's missing. Roman's going by
my place in the morning to look for it. Don't remember
losing it in the scuffle…

Her engagement ring? Could the chain have come un-
clasped at some point? The last time he'd noticed it was
when they'd first arrived at the hospital and it had slipped
out from under the neckline of her shirt.

He texted back, asking when she last remembered
having it, but she hadn't responded by the time he finished getting ready to turn in. She'd probably already
fallen asleep.

Luke climbed into bed and reached over, switching
off the bedside lamp. Tomorrow he'd look around the
hospital waiting room and Triss's room, make sure the
cars Natalie had ridden in were thoroughly checked. But
something was nagging him. It had been nagging him
since the first attack. Natalie's ring was the most valuable item she'd had with her in Mexico. Some might be
led to believe it was worth far more than the purported
six grand. He grabbed his phone and did a quick search,
verifying that copycats could run up to fifty grand. Was
it possible her attackers were after the ring?

Even if that were the case, Natalie would have noticed
the chain being ripped from her neck, right? He set the

phone down and rolled onto his side, trying to put the matter out of his mind until morning. Minutes ticked by slowly, and he felt more awake by the second. Finally, he got back out of bed, changing again. He'd just run over to Natalie's place and take a look around. She'd fought back hard. It was possible she'd lost it in the chaos. And if someone was after the ring, he could return to complete the search.

Luke knew that Roman had beefed up Natalie's security system, so it was highly unlikely anyone would successfully gain access. But he also knew himself. Once he got an idea in his mind, he had to see it through. He'd run over there, look for the ring and then he'd be able to sleep.

Luke had been right about one thing: the ring was in Natalie's apartment. He'd been wrong about the other: sleep hadn't come easily just because he'd located it. Making sure the zipper pocket on the inside of his jacket was securely fastened, he got out of his car. Operating on little sleep had never been a big deal to him, but he'd barely grabbed four hours after the ring hunt—which wasn't going to do him much good on the night shift later.

An involuntary yawn rose up as he unlocked the door of the old brick building he'd been renovating for the past couple of months. He couldn't be doing this kind of stuff. He knew better. He'd spent nearly every waking hour on Kendra's case—both on and off duty. He recognized the signs of attachment, and knew that his 2:00 a.m. ring hunt had been overkill.

Even Roman had questioned him on it when he'd messaged him to let him know he'd found the ring. In fact, Roman had seemed more interested in discovering what had possessed Luke to go in search of the ring than in what Luke had found.

And what Luke had found was the intact ring, mixed up with a pile of decorative items that had spilled out of one of the toppled boxes. Farther across the room, he'd found the broken chain, noted the stretched-open links, obviously pointing to the idea that the intruder had yanked the chain from Natalie's neck. She claimed she didn't recall that, but then again, adrenaline and shock often had the maddening ability to alter and even erase critical memories. Was this ring the target after all? Several boxes in the room had been sliced open. Maybe not. The intruder had been looking for something, and he had to have known that Natalie hadn't been back to her apartment since the wedding day. The ring couldn't have been in any of the boxes that had been rifled through.

He started a slow walk-through of the building, forcing away questions about the ring and mentally cataloging his plan of action for the week. Roman had Natalie's situation covered, and Luke would be dropping the ring off at the Harper estate in a little bit. Even Triss seemed to be squared away, and would possibly be discharged in the next day or two. Luke had dropped by the hospital on the way to the building. Triss's quick recovery wasn't the only surprise that had been waiting for him there. Hunter Knox had been in the hospital room with her—and not as an assigned guard. As a friend. Luke wondered if there was something there he hadn't recognized before, but he didn't give it much thought. Hunter was a nice guy, whose wife had died a couple of years ago. He was probably just doing the right thing and keeping her company.

What Luke needed to concentrate on was his nonprofit. For the next hour, he walked the building, checking in with the construction crew, giving directions and answering questions. The initial repairs were nearly done, and several columns of old library bookshelves had already been torn out, a full kitchen going in. The next plans to consider were for the installation of a basketball court and a small chapel. Luke was taking measurements and making notes when a text from Roman popped up on his phone.

Finished at the station. Change of plans. Coming to you for the ring.

Luke pocketed his phone and then finished up a few measurements. He'd recently come across an ad for old pews a church was getting rid of, and he thought he might be able to update them with cushions to bring traditional and modern together in the chapel while also maximizing seating. He put in a phone call, leaving a message about his interest in the pews, and then headed back toward the front of the building, where the sun was beaming in from the new oversize windows he'd had installed.

The morning was disappearing fast, the sun bursting out on a nearly cloudless day. This was exactly where he was supposed to be. He still felt a loyalty to Shield, and he'd work for Roman on a part-time basis for a while, but this community center would fill a hole Luke had been trying to fill since his own lonely middle-school years. And it would also provide a much-needed distraction from his growing attraction to Natalie.

But then the Shield SUV pulled up, and Roman emerged, coming around to the passenger side to open the door for Natalie.

She wore a dark pair of jeans with a floral blouse that made her seem even younger, her blond hair styled into silky straight, wispy layers, a pair of simple silver hoop earrings finishing the look. Luke opened the building door for them and Natalie smiled toward him, but the expression didn't reach her eyes, her skin pale enough to fade yesterday's sunburn.

"You didn't need to get out of the car," Luke said, even as the pair walked into the building. "I would have come to you." He looked from one face to the other, sensing he'd missed something big at the police station. "How'd the interview go?"

Roman looked to Natalie, and she shrugged—a gesture that was clearly disproportionate to whatever she was feeling.

"Let's see," she began, faint sarcasm in her tone. "With the exception of footage from the bank where he withdrew all of his savings not long after he texted me, Kyle still hasn't been seen since the morning of the wedding. He's massively in debt, there's blood at his apartment and someone traveled on the plane with me using Kyle's stolen credit card and passport. Airport video surveillance shows it was not, in fact, Kyle. So, of course, the police wanted to go down the line of questioning that included my possible involvement in Kyle's disappearance and a potential plan to run off with this unknown man."

Luke shook his head, trying to piece all the details together. "What motive would you have?"

"The list of Kyle's affairs is impressive. The police assumed I knew. To be fair, I must have been blind not to."

"What proof do they have?"

"None," Roman said. "Which is why they had to let her go."

Luke started to ask about the blood in the apartment, but Natalie had turned away from them, taking in their surroundings. "Wait a minute," she said. "Is this the building you were telling me about? For the community center?"

He nodded. "There's still a lot of work to do."

Her gaze traveled the entryway, curiosity in her expression. "Wow. Can you show me around?"

Luke paused, taking in the interest on Natalie's face and the guarded expression on Roman's. Roman had already visited more than once and had been very supportive of the venture, but every moment Natalie was away from home base put her at higher risk. Plus, truth be told, he felt a little protective of the old place. Right now it was just a shell of an abandoned library that had caught fire and never been restored. He didn't expect anyone to see what he saw. "You've got enough going on right now. How about I invite you to the grand opening when it's all fixed up?"

Natalie shrugged, her eyes still troubled as she sent him a half-hearted smile. "I could use a distraction for a few minutes." She was already walking down the hall, so Luke had no choice but to follow.

He tried not to read too much into Natalie's interest in his project. How she could be facing so much personal trauma and still muster the energy to offer up encouragement on a new friend's business venture spoke to her selflessness.

She ran her hands along empty bookshelves, most of which would be torn down and repurposed over the next few weeks. Then she glanced over her shoulder at Luke. "What's your vision, Luke? I want to see it the way you do."

He couldn't pinpoint what had caused the squeeze in his heart—whether it was her words, her sincere interest or the perfect ray of sunshine that filtered through a window onto the place she was standing. Whatever the cause, he knew immediately that he shouldn't have invited her into his dream. It made him imagine what it might be like to dream together. But they were here now, and there was no turning back.

"Well, where you're standing right now will be converted into one of the common areas," he started. He described his vision quickly, touching on the most important details before cutting the tour short and circling back to the entrance. Natalie looked up at the high ceilings with the light filtering through, turning in a slow circle as if she were seeing the completed vision Luke had just described and then met his eyes again.

"I love it," she told him, beaming. "Count me in."

"It'll be a while before it's up and running."

"I'm pretty good with a paint roller," she said with a smile. "And I know a lot of people in the media, so I can help get you some publicity. That could lead to more donors."

Something stirred in Luke's soul, but he caught Roman's observant eye and reminded himself to stand down. Lots of people had offered to help him over the years, but few people ever actually stepped up to the plate. That knowledge had protected him from a boatload of disappointment in his life.

"Thanks," he said. "I'll keep that in mind. For now, you have enough to worry about."

They both knew it was true, but it also gave her an easy out, and he was prepared for her to take it.

NINE

"Oh, before you go," Luke said, reaching inside his jacket and producing her engagement ring and the chain she'd worn it on.

Natalie accepted the jewelry, inspecting the broken chain. "Must have been ripped off during the attack."

Luke nodded. "I looked up the original out of curiosity. Didn't realize how much some of the replicas go for."

"Natalie and I were just discussing that on the way here," Roman said. "Could be that someone thinks hers is worth more than it really is."

"You told me you never saw the papers," Luke said to Natalie. "Do you think it's possible it's worth more than Kyle told you? There's the debt…"

"I doubt it. Seems like he would have embellished how much it was worth, not undercut the cost. I called his mom to see if we could get into his apartment, find the appraisal paperwork. But she said the police confiscated everything."

"Right."

"My friend Hannah said she'd take a look at it in the morning. Her family owns the Timeless Treasures."

"Good plan." Luke crossed the entryway and opened the front door, scanning the street beyond. "Ready to head back?"

She nodded, following Roman outside as Luke closed the door behind them. Waving a quick goodbye, she ducked into the SUV and settled into the silence. It had been a full morning, and she had a lot to process. As if the lengthy police interview hadn't been enough, the phone call with Kyle's mom had been emotionally draining, as Cheryl Paxton had commented again and again how sorry she was that Kyle had left Natalie the morning of the wedding. She, of course, followed up her apologies with speculation that Kyle must have had important reasons. Kyle was the Paxtons' only child, so Natalie didn't take offense. They'd always been massively proud of him, so it only made sense that they'd rise to his defense.

But the more Cheryl had talked, the more emotional she had become, her thoughts circling back time and again to her son and where he'd disappeared to.

Natalie's stomach rolled. She'd thought since the beginning that Kyle had just taken off for a few days, but as more evidence poured in about his financial straits, his affairs and now her own questions about the ring, she had to seriously consider the idea of foul play.

Guilt flooded her conscience as she considered the possibility that Kyle may not have voluntarily left town. She'd spent so much time focusing on her anger that she hadn't really given much credence to the thought that he could be in danger. Whatever he had done—the affairs, the lies— he deserved justice, not death.

She recalled the images the police had shown her earlier in the day. Grainy images of the suspect who'd broken into her apartment—photos that a neighbor's camera had captured. There, a stranger stared back at her, one with olive skin, dark eyes and near-black hair that came to a sharp widow's peak. Short hair. Sharp nose. Her mind scrolled through footage pulled from airport security of the man who had boarded her plane using Kyle's travel documents.

How he'd gotten through security was a mystery. He and Kyle looked nothing alike. But when she'd asked that same question of one of the case officers, he'd pointed out their similar height and build. "Lots of people pass through security every day," he'd said. "If you have a valid ticket and identification, you could slip through."

Which, of course, begged more questions. Who were these men? Or did the photos capture the same man at two locations? What did he want from Natalie? And what did he have to do with Kyle? She couldn't naively keep assuming that Kyle was completely uninvolved. Not after she'd seen the photos of his destroyed apartment and the two smears of blood on the inside of his apartment door, the spatters of it on the edge of his white bathroom sink.

What a mess.

And it wasn't the only mess.

Her boss had texted her asking her to come in to work for a meeting tomorrow, and he sounded serious. She couldn't imagine what the purpose for the meeting could be, and that made her nervous. But at least she'd heard back from her landlord with good news earlier. She'd be able to renew her lease, which meant she wouldn't have the added pressure of trying to find a new place to live.

The SUV slowed as it closed in on the gated entrance of her father's property. A handful of news vans sat just outside the gate, reporters snapping photos of the vehicle as it passed. They wouldn't get anything usable with the dark tint of the windows, but their presence bothered her. That was one of the reasons she'd gone into public relations. She valued the opportunity to give people a chance to be in charge of what information went out to the public, how they wanted to be portrayed and how they wanted to respond to questions and allegations. She'd seen publicity at its worst when her brother was murdered, and while she supported the media as a whole, there was no question that sometimes they lacked ethics, tact and morals.

The electronic gate slid open, the SUV rolling slowly toward the front of the house. They'd moved here when Natalie and Kristin were young teens, and even though the house was enormous, it had never felt too big. Instead, it had felt like a new beginning. Her father had received a substantial settlement from the State of Maryland due to the fact that his son had been kidnapped on a field trip while under the supervision of the public education system. He'd used a portion of the money to set up a foundation supporting families of missing and exploited children, and the rest he had used to create this sanctuary of sorts.

Theirs was the house friends gathered at. Homecoming and prom after-parties were here, pool parties and barbecues and fire pits, slumber parties, and even community events once their father had met Stacy. They'd left behind the darkness from their old house, where they'd all grieved the loss of little Liam, where the screaming matches between their parents had echoed down the hallways and where Natalie and Kristin had come home from school to find their mother unconscious in the master bedroom, empty prescription bottles on her nightstand. And they'd started over again. The pain from the past could never be forgotten, and their father had never pretended it would be. But together, the three of them had made the commitment to learn how to live again.

The car stopped and Roman came around to the back, opening her door. The Amish rocking chairs sat empty on the wraparound porch Natalie had always loved. It had been years since she'd sat in one of those chairs to watch the sunrise and listen to the bird families and crickets, the swish of the treetops and the distant rumble of lawn-mowers on the property and trucks on the highway. For as long as she could remember, she'd sneak out of the house early in the morning, watching until the sun crested the trees just beyond the property—or until someone called her inside. She'd never been in a rush to get back to what awaited inside—chores, tutors, lessons and seemingly endless social engagements. Even though she'd enjoyed most of it, sometimes she'd longed to slow down enough to figure out her own thoughts.

There never seemed to be enough time for that. Life never really slowed down, she realized. She'd always told herself she liked it that way, but as she passed by the tempting rockers, a tug of longing surprised her. She'd spent the past couple of decades staying busy and sur-rounding herself with people, doing anything to avoid downtime and the inevitable silence that came with it.

To Natalie, silence was loud and torturous, filled with regret and fear and loneliness. Suddenly repelled by the idea of laying low for days at a time with nothing to do at her father's house, she slowed her strides. Next to her, Roman stopped.

"Everything okay?" he asked, his dark sunglasses hid-ing his expression.

She almost nodded and continued walking, so used to going along with everyone else's plans for the sake of peace. Instead, she stood her ground.

"To be honest, I don't like the arrangements," she said. "I'll drive myself crazy twiddling my thumbs at my dad's house for days on end."

"We can adjust the plan," Roman said. "What would make things easier for you?"

She tamped down the voice in her head telling her she

was being selfish or foolish, and decided to tell him exactly what she wanted. "I'd like to go back to work. And back to my apartment."

Roman was silent for several seconds, and Natalie braced herself for the inevitable shut-down that was coming.

"I get what you're saying," Roman said carefully. "But it'll be difficult for us to get a team together that fast." He took off his sunglasses and pocketed them, his dark eyes serious. "Tell you what. Let's devise a transition plan. We may need to keep you here a few more days, so we can get everything set up securely, but we'll get target dates and plans so the end will be in sight as far as getting you back to your place and back to work."

"That would be great," Natalie said, relieved. "In the meantime, maybe I can spend a few hours at my apartment unpacking this week so I'm ready to move back in."

"Sure," Roman said with a nod. "We can take you later this afternoon to get started, if you're up to it."

"I appreciate it, Roman. Thank you."

"We compromise when we can," Roman said lightly. "Clients still need to live normal lives." He turned and led the way up the porch, pulling the front door open for her.

Natalie quietly set her shoes in the foyer closet, eyeing her father's office. She had to pass it to get to the stairs. As much as she loved her dad, she didn't feel up to talking to anyone just now. Maybe he'd be so absorbed in his work, he wouldn't notice her walking past. She quietly padded along the wood floor, but the French doors were slightly ajar, and as she slipped past, he called to her.

"Natalie?"

She bit back her frustration and peeked her head inside the office, surprised to find he wasn't alone.

Her friend Julianna jumped up from where she'd been

sitting and rushed across the room to offer Natalie a hug. "I've been so worried about you." She stepped back, coffee-brown eyes sweeping over Natalie with concern.

"I tried to call you back, but—"

"Oh, I know. I got your messages. You just didn't sound like yourself, so I figured I'd check on you." She glanced over at Natalie's father. "Your dad's been filling me in. How are you holding up?"

"I've been better," Natalie admitted, touched that Julianna had gone out of her way to visit, but wishing she could just have some time to herself.

"Sit for a few minutes," her dad said from his leather recliner near the bay window. It was where he'd sat every morning for as long as Natalie could remember, a Bible in his lap, a pen in his hand. This afternoon, the Bible sat closed on the table, his glasses sitting on top.

Natalie was tired, but she wasn't rude, so she dragged a chair across the floor toward him, resigned to the fact that she would have no peace until she'd told him every detail of her day. At least Julianna was there so she wouldn't have to repeat it all later.

Julianna swept around the small round table to take her own seat, strappy heels clicking on the hardwood floor. She wore skinny jeans and a sleeveless crimson top that flowed gently over her barely detectable baby bump. Just over four months pregnant, she was still the epitome of fashion, her long dark waves spilling over her bare shoulders and halfway down her back, her makeup flawless. She and Natalie couldn't be more different, but they'd forged a friendship, anyway.

Julianna's story was an interesting one—a runaway discovered by a talent scout, she'd risen from a life of poverty and abuse to pursue an acting career, and from her success, she had poured an enormous amount of time and money into mental health awareness, an issue that was close to Natalie's heart, particularly because of her own mother's suicide.

To some, Julianna seemed shallow. Her marriage to a wealthy senator nearly twice her age didn't cast a flattering light on her. But Natalie had gotten to know her well over the past year that they'd been working together, and had come to think of her as a good friend.

"You look downright exhausted," Julianna said. "I feel like I didn't pick a great time to come."

That was Natalie's chance, if she wanted to speak up for herself. She could simply tell both her father and Julianna that she needed a break. But she found herself shaking her head and drumming up a smile instead, like she always did. "No, it's okay. I'm glad you're here."

The recap of the day took more than an hour, with her lawyer-turned-judge father asking ten questions for every statement Natalie made, while Julianna spent a lot of time shaking her head in disbelief and sympathy. As much as she had wanted to go straight to her room when she got back to her dad's place, there was something therapeutic about rehashing the details again, about turning the events around and looking at every angle.

Eventually, though, she'd relayed everything she could remember, and weariness started setting in again. Julianna seemed to sense it. "What a nightmare," she said with a sigh, pushing away from the table. "I wish I could stay longer, but I'm glad you're with family for now. It's no time to be alone."

She stood, and Natalie followed suit. "I'll walk her out," she told her father, and the two made their way out of the office and toward the foyer.

"Thanks for coming by," Natalie said at the door. "It meant a lot."

"I'm just glad you're okay." Julianna paused before reaching for the door, uncertainty flashing in her eyes. "Before I go…"

She hesitated, and Natalie waited, curious. Julianna was generally pretty outspoken and not one to hesitate.

"Well, the timing feels wrong, but I wanted to give you a heads-up about the meeting tomorrow."

"My work meeting?" Natalie asked, wondering why Julianna would have insider knowledge on it.

Julianna nodded. "It's not my decision at all," she started to explain, and disappointment began to grow in the pit of Natalie's stomach. She knew immediately she wouldn't like what Julianna had to say. "Because of all the publicity over the weekend… You know, with Kyle missing and…"

Her voice trailed off, and Natalie just nodded.

"Marcus—you know how much I can't stand the man?" Julianna continued.

Again, Natalie nodded, knowing exactly where this was heading. Marcus, with seven more years than Natalie invested in the PR company, had been livid about the possibility of being passed up for partner, and he'd made it known.

"Well, he suggested to Chris that he temporarily take over on the publicity for the fund-raiser, and it looks like Chris is in agreement."

That Marcus had suggested such a thing didn't surprise Natalie. But that her boss would even consider it? That worried her.

"We've been planning for months," Natalie said. "It would take a lot to catch him up to speed. We have media interviews scheduled for next week. He wants to just take over?"

Julianna raised her eyebrows in agreement. "Exactly. I thought you'd want to know ahead of time."

"I appreciate it," Natalie said, but the news had hurt. Would Chris really let Marcus convince him? She had to admit that her position wasn't ideal to be fielding all the publicity logistics for the event, but she was confident she could make it work. She'd just have to convince her boss of that.

"I'm sorry," Julianna said, her voice soft. She hugged Natalie and reached for the door. "Want to have lunch at my place tomorrow before your meeting? Maybe we can talk about a plan."

"Sure, thanks."

Julianna pulled the door open to leave, but instead of waving goodbye to Natalie, she quickly took a step backward into the foyer. "Hello," she said in surprise.

"Ms. Montgomery, right?"

Natalie's heart leaped at the sound of Luke's voice, her pulse racing when he came into view.

"Yes." Julianna extended a hand.

"I'm Luke Everett, with Shield. Pleasure to meet you."

"You, as well."

Luke's attention shifted to Natalie. "I don't want to cut your visit short…"

"I was on my way out, Luke," Julianna said smoothly, turning to send a good-natured eyebrow lift toward Natalie. "I'll see you tomorrow, okay?"

Natalie nodded, wondering what Luke was doing here. Roman had said he'd taken the day off to work a double that night and into tomorrow.

Luke stepped inside and closed the door. "Ella's in labor, so I'm taking over for Roman."

"They must be so excited," Natalie said, thinking back

to the tenderness she'd observed between the two at the hospital.

"Roman's not generally an excitable person, but this is definitely an exception," Luke said with a grin.

Then, his expression grew more serious. "He tells me you're determined to get some normalcy in your life. Can't say I blame you. The team's ready to bring you over to your apartment for a couple hours whenever you're ready."

"Great," Natalie said, still reeling from his sudden appearance at the house. "I'll be ready in ten minutes."

She hurried up to her room to change into workout capris and a soft tunic shirt, all the while fighting mixed emotions. She'd been only relieved when Roman had offered to bring her to her apartment. Why did it feel so much more personal to have Luke accompany her as she unboxed her life and settled it all back into place in drawers and on shelves?

She shook her head, not willing to spend time with those thoughts. Dragging a comb through her hair, she left her room, heading back downstairs to meet up with the team.

Luke was waiting at the front door, and Natalie pulled a pair of sneakers out of the closet, bending down to tie the laces quickly. When she stood, Luke touched the bandage peeking out from the neckline of her shirt, and her skin flushed at the contact. "How's your shoulder, by the way?"

"Could be worse," Natalie responded as Luke opened the door for her. "How's your sister?" She climbed into the back seat of the SUV. Carson was driving, next to an agent Natalie had not yet met.

The two nodded a greeting. "Hi Ms. Harper, I'm

Bryan," the man in the passenger seat said, a friendly smile on his face.

"Nice to meet you," she returned, buckling in as the vehicle pulled away.

"Triss is doing pretty well, actually," Luke said, returning to their conversation. "She might be released tomorrow morning. Just waiting for a few test results."

"This waiting," Natalie said with a sigh, wishing futilely for life to go back to normal again. "I'm not very good at it."

"I don't know many people who are," he said. "We like immediate answers, quick fixes. Waiting forces us to rely on faith, which feels a bit abstract at times."

Natalie hadn't had to wait on much in life. She'd had most things handed to her before she even realized she needed them. School trouble? Her parents hired a tutor. Bullying? She was sent to a psychologist. Growth spurt? New designer clothes. Career crisis? Her father and Stacy had laid out a plan for her and offered enough money for an education that would help her attain her goals.

She'd worked hard to achieve what she had, but the path had been paved for her, and it had been much easier for her than for a lot of her friends.

Maybe that's why this newest trouble seemed so daunting.

No one could sort things out for her. No one could give her any easy answers. Kyle was not about to reappear, claiming some enormous misunderstanding.

"If this is a lesson in faith, I think I'm failing miserably," she said.

Luke looked at her for a moment, as if deciding how to answer, but then his hand covered hers on the seat between them, warm and comforting. Her heart raced as his thumb brushed tenderly along the top of her wrist, spreading a flutter of awareness in its wake.

"I find it hard to believe you could fail miserably at anything," Luke said.

Guilt edged at her mind and she slipped her hand away from his, reaching into her purse for a piece of gum. "I could write you a list." She had failed with Kyle. She had failed with her relationships before him, too. Not to mention— where was Kyle? Was he running from someone? Who? Had his wedding-day skip-out been motivated by self-preservation rather than selfishness?

She wasn't exactly winning right now. If she'd been stronger, she would have left Kyle a long time ago. If she'd been savvier, she would have caught on to his affairs.

"Making mistakes is just part of living," Luke said. "We fail when we don't keep trying."

She sighed. "I just wish I had—"

"How about you don't go down that path, Natalie? Hindsight is twenty-twenty. Foresight is not."

She eyed Luke's profile. He'd been strong at every turn. Certain. He'd mentioned his faith as a driving force in his life. If that was the truth, then Natalie wanted to know more.

Luke didn't like the plan to move Natalie back into her apartment, but he also couldn't fault her for wanting to start getting her home back in order. She couldn't live in her parents' house indefinitely.

At least a crew had already come and gone, upgrading and activating the security system. And as they pulled up to the curb a while later, he had to admit that securing Natalie's tiny apartment would definitely be a much easier undertaking than securing her father's massive home.

Stepping out of the vehicle, Luke surveyed the street as he walked around to Natalie's door. The street was quiet, the rows of colorful homes peaceful. He wasn't one to take chances, though, and quickly escorted Natalie up to her front door, placing a hand at her back to keep her close.

He felt more at ease when they finally stepped into her apartment. With Carson in the car and two team members outside keeping an eye on the entrances, he knew Natalie would be safe.

"Where do you want to start?" he asked as they stood amid towers of boxes in her living room, her very fluffy cat weaving between their legs and purring loudly.

Natalie bent down and scratched the cat behind his ear, then crossed the living room to the office. "Here would be good."

It was a den, really, with two steps down into a space smaller than a hundred square feet. The furniture was modular and practical, her desk facing out the window that overlooked the street. Three empty ladder bookshelves lined the wall.

Natalie pointed to a stack of boxes to the right of one of the shelves. "I think there are mostly pictures and books in this one, if you want to stack some on the shelves."

He lifted a box off the stack and set it on the desk before his gaze strayed out the window to the street below. Across the street, an older couple sat on their porch in white rocking chairs. Natalie's view included a corner bakery and a pizza shop bookending the street. But beyond, he could see the Baltimore city skyline, and to the east some of the harbor. It was no wonder she wanted her apartment back.

Luke cut open the box and started pulling out books, lining them up one after the other on her bookshelves.

"Not for you, Taser." Next to him, Natalie laughed, lifting her cat from a pile of cords he'd sprawled out on top of, nibbling on one.

"Great name," Luke said, amused.

"When he was tiny, he would pounce on me out of nowhere and latch on. Those razor kitten claws are killers. Taser seemed to fit."

Luke laughed at that, and they fell into companionable silence as they unpacked until Luke came across a handful of tissue-wrapped flat parcels.

He lifted one out and unwrapped it. It was a photo framed in black with an ivory matte. Natalie and her sister from younger days, looking so identical he almost couldn't tell them apart. He peered closer. In the photo, they wore blue-and-yellow track uniforms, their hair pulled back.

"Senior year of high school," Natalie said, glancing up from her own work.

"You're the one on the left," he said, though how he could tell, he wasn't sure.

"Impressive." She smiled as she pulled a box off a pile and set it on the floor, slipping a pocketknife along the tape to open it.

He set the frame on her desk so she could decide where she wanted to put it later, then pulled out the next one.

"Oh." Natalie's voice caught as the tissue came off and revealed a photo of her and Kyle.

By all accounts, they looked in love. It was a professional photo. Engagement, he guessed. Her left hand rested on Kyle's shoulder, the ring a gaudy focal point. The photo had been posed with the Inner Harbor behind them, the sun glimmering off the water as the two smiled inches apart.

"I'm sorry," he offered, handing the frame to her.

She stared down at it. "Can you pass me that tissue paper again? I think for now, I'll put things like this away."

He passed her a piece and continued sorting through the box, shelving books and setting out photos. In his periphery, Taser purred loudly, rubbing his cheek against the corner of the box Natalie had been about to unpack. Next to the box, Natalie sat on the floor, staring down at the framed photo, tissue ready to pack it up. She could tuck the memories away and hide the photographs, but she couldn't hide the grief in her eyes.

It was good that he'd forced some distance between them. Without a distraction, she could more easily process what she'd been through. He'd just keep telling himself that, because he hadn't been able to get her out of his mind.

In fact, the longer they worked together in the quiet and somehow intimate space of her den, unpacking items that told the story of her life, the more drawn to her he felt.

"No matter how a relationship ends, it's hard to say goodbye," Luke offered.

Natalie didn't look up from the photo. "I'm just wondering what I missed."

Breaking down the box he'd just emptied, he sat next to her on the floor, the couch at their backs.

"Some people are very good at pretending. Sometimes, there are no signs."

"I think there were. And that's the part I'll never understand. I saw the signs, and I was willing to ignore them. Why did I stay?"

"What signs?"

After hesitating, she asked, "Remember how I told you about the credit card?"

He nodded.

"We fought." Natalie's shoulders fell, her gaze breaking from his and settling on her hands in her lap.

"What happened?"

"After he explained the credit card thing, he said I should go home so he could cool off. I was heading out the door when it hit me that I'd never seen a new credit card in the mail."

"Usually the new card comes before the statement."

"Right."

Darkness flashed in her eyes, but she didn't look away. Luke had seen the look before—the shame in the eyes of a woman who'd been hurt, and who had stayed, anyway. Many of Shield's clients came from situations like that.

"I circled back to the kitchen. Demanded an explanation. He stood up and told me he didn't need to hear any more of my questions. What he needed was for me to get out of his house."

"Did you leave?"

"He pushed past me. I couldn't get out of his way fast enough. My head hit the edge of a framed painting." Her hand came to the back of her head. "Made a pretty good gash."

"What'd he do?"

"He helped me up, got me ice," she continued. "Apologized. Said he wasn't himself, that work had been stressful." Her cheeks were pink and she looked up at Luke again. They sat close, arms touching. "I should have left then."

"After that, how did he treat you?" he asked.

Natalie smiled sadly. "Like gold. I should have left, anyway. I'm not sure why I didn't."

"Love makes things cloudy sometimes."

Natalie shook her head. "I'm not even sure it was love

that kept me there. I guess I felt like it was too late. I'd made a commitment."

"You were loyal," Luke said.

"To a fault."

"There are worse things." He looked straight into her eyes, realizing the zing of chemistry between them, the soft warmth of her arm against his. "If you're going to be hard on yourself for something, don't let it be loyalty. Kyle's the one at fault. He's the one who messed this up. He's the one who loses in the end."

Natalie looked down at the photo and then around at the half-unpacked room, clutter everywhere. "Somehow it feels like I'm the one losing," she said.

She had a point, considering the past few days. She looked defeated, and it broke Luke's heart. All he'd seen of Natalie was strength and fortitude, and now it seemed as if she were reaching her breaking point.

"Hey," he said gently, and she turned her face toward him, eyes sad and glistening. He was going to tell her all the reasons she wasn't losing, all the reasons she was better off without Kyle Paxton. But somehow, the words wouldn't come, the air charged with undeniable chemistry.

He lowered his head toward her, against all better judgment, pausing just short of her mouth. She didn't turn away, and he *couldn't* turn away. For better or for worse, his lips brushed hers, tasting the sweetness of a tentative new beginning. That was all he meant to do, but then she tilted her head up and turned more fully toward him, her hand slipping onto his chest, and he deepened the kiss, forgetting all his reasons for staying away. At that moment, none of those reasons seemed to matter in the least.

TEN

This. This is what Natalie had been missing, and she'd never known it. She leaned into Luke's kiss, aware of the tender stroke of his fingers along the side of her neck, the rapid beat of his heart under her hand. She shifted closer to him, sliding her hand up behind his neck even as reality started to edge in. One year alone, she'd promised herself. But Luke pulled back for a moment, his eyes searching hers, and she knew she was lost. Heart beating frantically, she played with the hair at the nape of his neck, her eyes fluttering closed as he brushed his lips to the tip of her nose, her cheek, the sensitive skin near her ear, before finding her mouth again.

It wasn't just chemistry that had forged this connection, and Natalie knew it. Somehow, she could be herself with Luke in a way she hadn't allowed herself to be with anyone in a very long time. She felt safe with him. And for the life of her, she couldn't think of any reason to keep the promise she'd made herself.

A loud knock interrupted them, and she jumped, pulling back from the kiss and glancing toward the entryway, where Hunter stood alert in the open doorway. He'd obviously knocked to get their attention, and heat flushed up her neck and to her cheeks.

If Hunter had any judgment to pass, he did a good

job of keeping it hidden. Saying nothing about what he'd clearly walked in on, he stepped inside and shut the door behind him, his expression serious.

"Kyle's outside. I've already called the police."

Natalie's heart tripped and she stood, her mind fighting to focus on Hunter's announcement and let go of the kiss that still lingered on her lips.

Luke stood up next to her. "What does he want?"

"Says he just wants to talk to Natalie."

"No way," Luke said. "He doesn't get anywhere near her."

It was a statement of what should have been fact, but the truth was that Natalie had a lot of questions for her ex, and she wanted answers before he had a chance to disappear again.

"No. I'll talk to him."

Luke turned to her, not even trying to hide his surprise. "Let's let the police talk to him first."

His voice had a hard edge she hadn't heard before, and Natalie almost backed down. Maybe it was the strength she'd gotten from surviving so many close-calls in the past couple of days, or maybe it was the courage she had gleaned from confronting Roman about her security arrangements, but somehow she found her voice.

"I want answers," she said simply, staring determinedly back at Luke and noting a barely concealed flash of anger. She turned to Hunter. "You can bring him up."

She noticed the smallest hesitation, as if he wanted to suggest otherwise, but instead he nodded and left the apartment.

Luke crossed the room and parked himself on a stool at the kitchen bar top, facing the living room.

After the kiss they had just shared, the meeting felt like it might be awkward. She didn't ask Luke to leave, though. She wasn't worried for her safety, but she just felt stronger with Luke, regardless of how angry he seemed to be at the moment.

The door swung open and Kyle walked in.

The first thing she noticed was the bruise on his cheek. It was light, as if it had been healing for several days. But on Kyle's pale skin, it was noticeable and surprising.

The second thing she noticed was the anxiety in his expression—an emotion she'd rarely seen on him. His eyes locked on hers and he quickly covered the distance between the door and the living room, his arms opening to offer a hug. "Natalie," he said. "I'm so sorry."

She stepped back, avoiding the hug, uncertainty sweeping over her as his arms dropped in defeat. He tucked his hands into the pockets of his khakis, which were wrinkled and worn, as if he'd been living in them for a couple of days. He hadn't shaved in days, either, which was highly unusual for him. Kyle had always been meticulous about his appearance, almost too meticulous at times.

She waited, silently, for an explanation.

He looked around the room, his gaze darting from Natalie to Hunter to Luke. "Could we maybe have a little privacy?" he asked.

Luke shook his head, arms crossed. "No."

Hunter didn't budge from his place at the door.

Kyle's attention swerved back to Natalie, a nervous smile on his lips. "Bodyguards?" he asked lightly. "You know I'd never hurt you."

He already had, but Natalie wasn't about to go there. "Why are you here, Kyle? And where have you been?"

He looked hurt by her coldness, and Natalie felt a tug of sympathy she wanted to reject. He didn't deserve her sympathy. Not after what he'd done to her. But his disheveled appearance and the bruise under his eye spoke to a problem far beyond a simple case of cold feet. She glanced at Luke, but he didn't meet her eyes. Every ounce of his attention was focused on Kyle, as if he expected her ex to attack her at any moment. He did look unpredictable, his eyes a little wild. But Natalie didn't think he would try to do anything to her.

He sat down on the plastic-wrapped couch, and Natalie sat on a nearby chair.

"There's no excuse for what I did," he started, his eyes pleading. "But I'd backed myself into a corner, and I…I guess I just panicked."

"What do you mean you backed yourself into a corner?"

"I've never been good with money," he said, sliding a distrustful look over to Luke and then to Hunter. He clearly didn't want to have this conversation in front of them, but Natalie didn't have any intention of being alone with him.

"The inheritance?" she prodded.

"Pretty much gone," he admitted. "I didn't want to tell you. Didn't want to disappoint you."

"So you left me on our wedding day and disappeared for days with no explanation?" His words didn't ring true. "And what about your apartment? And someone using your passport and credit card?"

"I don't know about any of that. Someone must have broken in after I left town. I needed to get away for a while, clear my head. Like I said, I panicked. Didn't know what to do."

"You could have told me the truth," Natalie pointed out, though she wasn't sure what she would have done with the information.

"I should have. I know that now. I tried to make some of it back. Got sucked into some online gambling." He rubbed a hand over his face, regret shadowing his eyes. "The more I tried to fix it, the worse things got." His bloodshot eyes stared into hers, willing her to…what? Understand? Forgive? Give him another chance?

"But what you've heard about affairs… None of it's true." He reached out and took her hand, but she pulled it away. He dropped his head for a moment, and when he gazed back up at her, he looked lost, his eyes red-rimmed. "I never would have done that. I didn't want to lose you."

His brokenness stirred up emotions in Natalie that she had promised herself not to expend on him. She straightened. "Three different women have made claims about affairs with you," she pointed out. "You want me to believe they all made it up? What motive could they have?"

"Publicity? Shock factor? I don't know. I've never even met one of the women." He shook his head, as if in disbelief. "I haven't so much as looked at another woman since we met. I knew almost from day one that you were the one for me. And I know I messed up. But I still love you, Natalie. I want to make it up to you."

She was shocked silent for a minute, wondering why he would come back now, why ask for forgiveness, why expect she would offer it.

She shook her head. "I don't believe you, Kyle," she said flatly, glancing up at Luke, whose attention was fixed, distrusting, on her ex.

Kyle leaned closer, hopeless desperation in his eyes. "I'll prove it to you. Give me another chance?" he asked softly, and his voice reminded her of the way he'd spoken to her in the early months of their relationship, tender and charming and wooing. "You've always been too good for me, but you make me a better person," he continued. "You always have. It's why I chose you, why I need you."

He reached for her hand again, and for some reason,

she didn't retreat. She was certain he wasn't telling the truth, but his desperation was compelling. What had really happened to Kyle? She was in no way tempted to give him another chance, but she was concerned for his safety, for his health. Had he had a mental break? Was he in some sort of trouble he was keeping from her?

"You should have talked to me," she finally said, and no one in the room was more surprised than she when her voice cracked, her eyes suddenly stinging with tears. She willed the tears away, but her voice was broken as she whispered, "You handled everything in the worst possible way."

His hand dropped away, his shoulders drooping. Then he nodded slowly, as if accepting the sting of rejection. "Maybe in time…"

She said nothing as she stood and motioned toward the door.

He rose as well, standing still for a moment, as if trying to come up with a better argument, as if surprised she had stood her ground. But then he walked toward the door as she opened it, Hunter stepping to the side but keeping his attention fixed on Kyle.

At the entryway, Kyle stopped, his eyes pleading.

"You've always been a forgiving person," he said, his voice suddenly soft. "If you won't take me back, will you at least consider returning the ring? I'm in pretty bad shape right now…"

The request surprised her. She didn't know if she really felt like she had a right to the ring, especially if he needed the money. But she wouldn't be pressured. "I need some time," she told him, and opened the door wider for him to leave.

After the barest hesitation, he nodded slowly. "We can talk again tomorrow. Please. Just think about it."

"Let's go," Hunter said finally. "The police are outside, and they have questions for you."

Natalie watched for a couple of moments as Hunter escorted Kyle down the stairs to exit the building. Her ex almost looked like a different person entirely. Even the way he carried himself was different, shoulders low and head down.

How much of what he'd told her was the truth? And what was he still hiding from her?

Luke reached past her to close and lock the door, and wistfully she wished she could erase the past ten minutes and pick up right where she had left off—wrapped up in a moment with Luke she would probably remember for the rest of her life.

She glanced around the cluttered den, silently debating if she should call it quits. Between Luke's kiss and Kyle's sudden appearance, she was frazzled, to say the least. But she was here now with plenty left to get done, so she grabbed another box and tore it open.

Taking Natalie's cue, Luke slid another box out and began to sort through the contents. But even as he carefully set books and knickknacks in place on shelves, he fought back a rising sense of anger. Anger, and—if he was honest with himself—hurt.

He remembered the moment when Hunter had told them Kyle had arrived—the mixture of surprise and relief he'd noted on Natalie's face. Then there was the moment Kyle had set his hand on hers and she hadn't pulled away, the few extra seconds she had taken before pushing him to leave. The way she'd looked sadly at her ex and told him she needed time to think. Was she actually considering another chance with Kyle? And what about the ring? Why not just give it back? It wasn't like she or her father really needed the money. Did she want to keep it out of spite, or sentiment?

Maybe it wasn't any of his business, but as hard as he tried to convinced himself he was just worried for her, worried that she could be fooled by Kyle's smooth words and charm like he'd obviously been fooling her for over a year, he knew his own feelings ran deeper than that.

Against all better judgment and against all experience had taught him, he'd let down his guard with Natalie in a matter of days. He'd let himself hope again, beyond all hope, only to come face-to-face with one crushing truth: she didn't feel the same way he felt.

They worked silently for a time, maybe both lost in their own thoughts, or maybe both unsure how to proceed after the eventful afternoon.

Finally, Luke spoke up. "You're quiet."

She situated another picture frame on her bookshelf and reached back into the box she was unpacking. "Just processing."

"What do you think about Kyle's story?"

"I don't think he's telling me everything."

"He didn't give a lot of concrete details," Luke agreed. "How do you feel, after seeing him again?"

"I don't know," she answered softly.

"It would make sense if you still had feelings for him," he said carefully, thinking through how he could point out Kyle's untrustworthiness. "You've been together awhile. And he's obviously going through something right now, so maybe you feel like you should be there for him, but just be careful."

"He'll have to find someone else to be there for him, because it won't be me."

She spoke with conviction, but Luke knew better. Natalie had been much kinder to Kyle than he had deserved.

He seemed to have some sort of smooth charm that could easily manipulate Natalie's emotions.

"Now that he's back, what do you plan to do with the ring?"

She sighed. "I'll probably give it back."

That was a quick change from her original plan to sell it and pay her father back some of the wedding money. Just another sign that she still felt obligated to and somehow connected with the idiot who had humiliated her on her wedding day.

He stole a glance at Natalie's profile as he reached for another box. She seemed to be wholeheartedly concentrating on her task and purposely avoiding eye contact with him. A sinking feeling had followed him since Kyle had shown up and Natalie hadn't turned him away. Anyone on the outside looking in would say the guy didn't deserve five seconds with Natalie, yet she'd allowed him up, tried to hear him out. And while she hadn't exactly jumped happily into his arms, she hadn't given him the cold shoulder he'd expected her to, either.

And there was no denying the change in her demeanor from the moments before Kyle arrived to the half hour since. She was reserved, tense and all business, and Luke knew what that meant. He'd been here before, and despite the best intentions, he was right back in the place he'd been trying to avoid.

The same moment had played out with both Aimee and Kendra. Aimee had changed almost as soon as Triss had reappeared, nearly a year after she had run away. Kendra had changed overnight, once her case was closed and her hefty check was signed. They had both come to a moment in their lives where what they wanted in life veered off the track Luke had envisioned, and neither of them had ever looked back.

But looking back was a bad habit Luke had yet to conquer. Even nearly fourteen years after his mother's death, he replayed that last visit in his head from time to time—the way she had seemed distant, uninterested, unreachable.

On the opposite side of the small room, Natalie may as well have been a lifetime away from him for how distant she seemed. She broke down the cardboard box she'd just finished emptying and set it in the pile they'd made in the hallway. "I think I'm about done."

She met his gaze for the first time since Kyle had left, and what he thought he read there was loss. Weariness had settled over her features, her mascara lightly smudged under both eyes, wisps of hair escaping its elastic band.

Luke surveyed the room. "Only a couple of boxes left. Why don't you take a break and I'll finish up? Should only take a few minutes."

She shook her head. "No. I'll help. You're right. We're almost done. It'll feel good to have one room unpacked."

She grabbed one box, and he pulled the other one out. Methodically, they began to empty their boxes, side by side, and Luke was compelled to get the tension out of the air. They had made a mistake with the kiss. He knew it, and he was pretty sure she did, too. They were both adults, and there was no reason this had to continue to hang awkwardly in the air.

"I need to apologize," he said finally.

As if she hadn't heard, she continued her work, but her gaze flicked over to him, waiting for him to continue.

"Earlier…before Kyle came…I was out of line."

"If you're talking about the kiss, we were both involved," she said with a wry smile that didn't quite meet her eyes. "I wasn't exactly stopping you."

True. And it was a moment, a kiss, that would forever be seared into Luke's memory. For those few seconds, he'd let himself hope again, let himself believe in the possibility of a new beginning. "I shouldn't have started it. You're just days off of a broken relationship, and you and I have been through a lot of trauma together... Circumstances can trick people into believing in this—this... connection that isn't real." Even as the words rolled out, he fought the urge to backpedal. But he refused to fall back into his old pattern again, fighting for a one-sided love that wasn't meant to be.

Natalie nodded slowly, her expression veiled. "It's not a big deal, Luke. It was just a kiss."

Her words stopped him cold. He had done this his entire life—invested deeply in every relationship, and more often than not found that the feelings weren't mutual. Sometimes, the feelings weren't even comparable. It had not been just a kiss to Luke. It had been the dawning of what he had been longing for, the spark of a relationship he had started to fool himself into believing could transcend circumstances.

"Just so we're on the same page," he said in agreement, against the very draw of his own heart.

"Strange," Natalie said then, her attention easily pulled from their conversation. She showed him a cell phone that had been in her box. "It's Kyle's old phone."

"And?" He began to fold his now-empty box.

"He said he lost it."

"And somehow it wound up with your stuff?"

She shook her head. "Maybe. But Kyle packed the office himself. He came by my work and grabbed my key from me, said he was doing something nice for me. I came home and he'd boxed up the entire office. He had to have packed the phone."

It didn't seem like anything to be concerned about. Maybe he'd found the phone while packing up her apartment and hadn't wanted it to get broken, but hadn't needed it anymore. Maybe he'd forgotten to mention it to her.

"I wonder what we'd find if we charged it up," Natalie said. "It's probably got a password."

"Want me to see if our intern can get into it?"

"Sure, thanks."

He took the phone from her and pocketed it. She still cared enough about Kyle to want to see what he may have been hiding on his old phone. If Luke had had any doubts about her feelings, this squelched them.

"Let's head out," he said, leading her toward the door. He had a long shift ahead of him, and some thinking to do about whether he would stay on Natalie's case.

ELEVEN

Natalie flopped down on her childhood bed and stared up at the stark white ceiling, then around at the mint-green walls. She and her sister had spent many nights together in her room, staying up far too late and talking about friendship and boys and loss and dreams. She wished Kristin was here, but according to her father, it was looking like she'd be on bed rest for the remainder of the pregnancy. Stacy would be back from visiting her soon, but she could never fill in for Natalie's twin.

Natalie rolled onto one side. Her dad hadn't changed the room since she'd moved into a dorm at seventeen. Even the comforter was still the same, her high school awards still in frames on the walls. She couldn't decide if it felt good to be home, or sad, so she closed her eyes and tried not to feel at all.

But closing her eyes didn't shut out reality. Instead, it called up memories from the day that would not stop playing through her mind. Surprisingly, Kyle's sudden appearance at her apartment was not taking up the brunt of her emotional space. Her fingertips came to her lips as she recalled Luke's kiss, heart aching with the memory. Tears sprung to her eyes as his words echoed in her heart. *Not real?*

If what she'd been feeling for Luke wasn't real, then Natalie didn't know what was. Had he been so angry with her for letting Kyle up that he was willing to pretend their connection meant nothing? She swiped the tears away, reminding herself she'd vowed to stay away from men for a year. She'd barely lasted a couple of days. She only had herself to blame for putting herself out there, for trusting someone with her heart when she barely knew him.

She blinked into the darkness, the reality of the past few days hitting her hard. Restless, she flicked on her bedside lamp and climbed out of bed to rifle through her clothes. She grabbed a pair of workout capris and a black tank top, changing quickly and grabbing her phone and earbuds. Then she left the room, quietly closing the door behind her. The hall was dark, her socked feet silent on the wood floor as she headed to the stairs. Ahead of her, a form emerged from the stairwell.

She gasped, jumping back.

"Didn't mean to startle you."

"Jordan?" She blinked into the hall, her hand feeling along the wall for the light switch.

"Just doing the rounds," he said as her hand met the switch and light poured over them. "Didn't expect anyone but your dad to still be up. Everything okay?"

"Yes, thanks," she said, sidestepping him. "Getting a run in."

He nodded, moving past her into the hallway. "Don't work too hard."

It may have been a lighthearted jest, but Natalie was sure she detected sarcasm there. She glanced back over her shoulder as she headed down the stairs and saw him disappear down the hall.

She pushed aside the uneasy feeling that bubbled up. Jordan had undergone extensive background investigations and interviews. If Roman had vetted him, she could have confidence in him. She continued down the stairs and walked to the back of the house where the security office was located.

Tapping on the open door, she waited a beat and then walked in.

Hunter was at the monitors, and he turned to face her. "You're up late," he said with a smile.

"I'm going on a quick run," she told him, noting the immediate drop of his smile. "On the property," she added quickly. The Harper estate was gated, secured and monitored. She'd rather take the nature trail that started a half-mile down the road, but if she wanted to do that, she knew that a crew of Shield security members would be jogging with her, which would defeat the purpose of a nighttime run to clear her mind.

"Okay," he said. "Let me just call—"

"I want to run alone," she said, cutting him off. She knew she'd be up for a fight, but he just stared calmly at her, waiting for her to explain. "I'll stick to the garden trail. It's secure, and not that far from the house," she added.

He looked undecided. "Hold on a minute, okay?" He grabbed his radio. "Ms. Harper wants to do the garden-trail run. Requests no escorts. You okay with that?"

"Hold on. I'll be right there."

Luke's voice shouldn't have the effect on her that it did, but there was no denying the fact that her heart had flipped right into overdrive when she'd heard him.

Caught between the stubborn urge to head out on her run anyway and the alarming thrill of anticipation as she waited for him to appear, Natalie took a seat next to Hunter.

"Sorry," he offered. "Luke's the shift supervisor tonight. I don't call the shots."

She shrugged. "I get it."

Hunter tapped his fingers on the table and then grinned conspiratorially at her. "You know…you could just take off now and I could watch Luke run after you. That would make the rest of the shift go a lot faster."

Natalie laughed at the thought. "I don't know how anyone works this shift."

"Takes a little getting used to, but it's perfect for me. I work when the kids are sleeping, sleep when they're at day care, spend time with them in the afternoons and evenings."

Natalie had noticed he didn't wear a wedding band, and she was curious about his story. She was about to ask when Luke appeared at the door, and every thought fled her mind.

He managed to make a black pair of pants and a white button-down look comfortable, his shirtsleeves cuffed, his black tie just a little loose.

"Hi," she said, her throat suddenly dry.

"I'm fine with you going on a run, but you know I can't let you go alone."

Luke watched Natalie's response, realizing quickly she wasn't going to easily agree to his terms.

"The whole property is gated with motion detectors," she pointed out, as if he didn't already know that.

"I'm still not comfortable with it."

"How about if I cut the loop in half and do a few half-mile circuits so I'm closer to the house?"

Luke rubbed the back of his neck, torn. The truth was, she was right. The property was secure. He'd designed the Harper family's security system himself, and had overseen and inspected the installation. The trouble was, the *garden trail*, as the family called it, was more like an overgrown forest than a garden, filled with mazelike paths that he wouldn't exactly label trails. It would be difficult to monitor her every move.

But logic won out when he reminded himself that the entire property was secure.

"All right," he finally agreed. "We'll let the patrols know to keep an eye out for you, but not to follow."

She smiled, standing up and popping her earbuds in. "Thank you." With that, she brushed past him and headed out the back door.

Luke didn't like it. He didn't like it at all. He hovered stiffly over the monitors as Hunter alerted the property patrols to keep an eye out for Natalie but not interfere with her run. She stood at the edge of the property doing some quick stretches and Luke scanned the monitors. No one but the patrols.

Logically, Luke knew she was safe, despite the recent cutback on property patrols at the Harper estate. It seemed Judge Harper had finally come to the realization that his security obsession was just a hair over-the-top. The latest contract included two property patrols, two inside patrols and a surveillance monitor at all times. Really, he'd do just fine with the security system alone. It underwent weekly safety inspections, and emergency crews could be on-site within four minutes of an alarm trigger.

The judge couldn't be convinced, though. He'd spent so many years vigilantly overseeing the security of his property and loved ones that every change was difficult for him. For now, that was for the best. At any given time, one of the property patrols was on the garden side of the fifteen acres. If Natalie needed help, she'd get it quickly. But she wouldn't need help. If Luke had any doubt, he wouldn't have let her go. Well, she may still have decided to run, but she wouldn't have been able to stop his team from following her.

"Why don't you take a seat?" Hunter glanced up at him pointedly.

"I won't stay. I know you've got the monitors covered." Still, he hesitated.

"Won't offend me if you stay. Two pairs of eyes are better than one." He pulled out the chair next to him.

Luke sat. Not because he didn't trust Hunter's competence, but because it was the closest thing to protecting Natalie that he could do.

"I think she's starting to feel a little suffocated," Hunter said.

"Maybe, but she's a smart woman. She knows the kind of danger she's up against."

On the monitor, Natalie took off at a quick pace. She started her run on the far side of the property, where a winding dirt running path led into what was more like a mini forest than an overgrown garden.

"Whoever's after her isn't messing around," Hunter agreed. "Your sister was in bad shape." His demeanor changed as he said those words, and Luke glanced over at him, wondering just what kind of connection he and his sister had. Hunter had to be several years older than Triss, and with two kids already, it was not a situation Luke would have picked for her, regardless of how much respect he had for Hunter.

"Nice of you to visit her this morning," Luke said. "I wouldn't have expected that after the late night."

"Had to get up and get the kids to day care, anyway. Thought she might enjoy a visit. But I think she would have rather been alone." He half smiled, then looked back at the monitor screens. "She's fast."

Natalie had already nearly made it to the half-mile

mark. Luke guessed she wouldn't keep that speed for long, but maybe it was her normal pace. He noticed that one of the patrols was nearby, and that set his mind at ease—for about two seconds. Hadn't the guy just been near the house? He leaned closer to the screens, counting three patrols.

"Knox, there are three patrols on the ground."

"No, two."

"Exactly." Luke stood, pointing to the black suits on the monitors. "One, two, *three*." Heart slamming against his ribs, he got on his radio. "Patrols, verify locations."

He listened as two team members checked in with badge ID numbers and locations, hoping against all hope that it was just a scheduling mishap. But when the third patrol was silent, Luke knew he didn't belong. He reached over, bypassing the security codes and sounding the intruder alarm.

Picking up his radio again, he named the location of the unidentified person and called for all agents to head to the preserve. Maybe he was wrong. Maybe it was a scheduling error, and the guy had forgotten to turn his radio on. It was too dark to distinguish features, to know for sure whether or not he belonged there. But Luke didn't care if he was wrong. Better he be wrong than Natalie be dead.

TWELVE

Natalie had found her rhythm. This was the part she'd always loved about running. The in-between. The speed after the warm-up, the cool night breeze against her skin, the steady rise of her heart rate as her feet flew along the trail. The gardens had always been one of her favorite parts about the property. She imagined that decades ago a homeowner had dreamed up an elaborate garden that simply couldn't transfer from conception to soil. Weeping willows fought with apple and pear trees that never produced edible fruit; lilac bushes grew tall and overbearing, crowding out blackberry bushes and the occasional stray tomato plant that would pop up in the hot summer months. No matter what was going on at home, at school or at work, a walk or a jog through the gardens never failed to boost her spirits, different blooms and the mixed fragrances of flowers and fruit surprising her throughout the year.

She wouldn't be able to maintain this speed, but that was okay. She'd just cut back on the return loop. Music blasting through her earbuds, she could almost pretend it had been a normal day. That her missing ex had not showed up at her apartment, pleading for a second chance. That she had not shared a kiss with Luke that had ruined her for any other kiss. But as the song she was listening to slowed and quieted to an end, another sound rang through. An echo, high-pitched and squealing. Natalie yanked the earbuds from her ears, slowing her pace to listen.

An alarm, echoing from the main house and all around the property. Natalie stopped and whirled around, half expecting someone to emerge from behind a nearby tree. She turned in a quick circle, searching the shadows of the trees and bushes for anyone who might be lurking. Had something happened back at the house? Or was the alarm for her?

Suddenly extremely aware of every sound and shadow, Natalie started to jog back toward the house. Afraid to run at full speed on the chance that she might run directly into someone who didn't belong, she squinted into the dark, unable to hear anything beyond her footsteps, her breathing and the wailing alarm.

In her runner's belt, her cell phone vibrated. She yanked it out and saw a message from Luke.

Come back now. Run.

Phone clutched in her hand, she took off then. Luke could see the monitors. If he said to run, he must know something she didn't. She trusted him implicitly.

"Natalie!" a voice called from her right, and she jumped, slowing as she tried to make out the speaker. It was too dark to recognize the person, but she recognized the uniform. Black suit, black tie, white shirt. Relief poured over her as she switched direction.

"What's going on?" she asked. "Luke texted me—"

The man's arms came up then, a dark object in his hands, aimed at Natalie. She stumbled, heart tripping at the narrow gleam in his eyes. Whirling around, she took off toward the house again. She ran like she had never run before, gasping for breath as flashes of light followed her.

A silencer? She zigzagged away from the path, cutting through the gardens, anticipating the strike of a bullet.

"Natalie!" Voices beckoned her from up ahead. Footsteps. Safety. Bryan and another Shield agent she didn't recognize emerged from the shadows ahead almost simultaneously. They motioned her back toward the house where Hunter was running toward her, and they took off after the intruder. This time, whoever was after her wouldn't get away. There was no way the Shield team would let that happen. But she hoped no one would get hurt in the process.

Ahead, her father held the back door open, his stance rigid with anxiety. Hunter ushered her inside, and her father bolted the door behind her, wrapping his arms around her. "You're okay, you're okay," he whispered in her ear.

The assurance was meant for her, but she was certain by his tight grip that it was also for himself.

"This way." Hunter gestured toward the security office. "We'll secure you both," he said as he stepped inside with them and locked the door. Safe, but tense, Natalie watched the monitors. It appeared that the intruder had already been apprehended—two agents were forcing him through the gardens and back toward the house.

"Police are on the way," Hunter said. "Can't wait to find out who this guy is, and—"

He tensed and grabbed his radio.

"Luke. We have movement in Natalie's bedroom."

"Ten-four. We'll check it out."

Natalie stood, still recovering her breath, moving next to Hunter. "What's going on?"

Hunter pointed to a panel of numbers to the right of the screens. Several were lit up in red. The others were black. "Your bedroom is number eleven. Red means occupied.

No cameras in private rooms, of course, but motion detectors show us areas of concern if we need to investigate."

Luke and another agent appeared on the stairwell, heading up to the second floor. Natalie's dad had sidled up next to her, and they all watched silently, the air in the room thick as they waited for the men to make it to Natalie's room.

Stealthily, they crept down the hallway, guns drawn.

"Be advised," Hunter said into his radio. "Door's locked from inside."

The men paused just outside the door to Natalie's bedroom.

"I didn't lock it when I left," she whispered, as if she were standing right there in the hall with them.

Natalie stared hard at the screen as the two men prepared to enter.

"He's with Nick. The guy's been around since day one. They know what they're doing," Hunter said, his voice sure as he pushed a chair over to her.

She took the seat he offered, suddenly feeling unsteady, her emotions hitting every extreme. Who was in her room, and why? And what was going to happen when the door opened?

Luke waved Nick back, standing motionless at the door, listening.

A shuffling movement sounded from within, followed by the definite slide of a drawer opening, then closing.

Someone was in there, all right, and they were about to find out who.

Luke reached for the doorknob, looking to Nick for agreement. He nodded. Swiftly, Luke slid the master key in the knob and swung the door inward—and right into Jordan Skehan's surprised face.

"Whoa," Jordan said, putting both hands up in defense.

Luke lowered his gun just slightly. "What are you doing in Natalie's room?" he demanded, trying to make sense of the situation. He'd imagined several scenarios, but none of them had included a Shield agent in Natalie's bedroom.

Nick moved closer to Luke so they were shoulder to shoulder in the doorway.

Jordan's eyes widened, his stance very still. Caught.

"Don't get trigger-happy now," he said with a tight smile. "I just thought I'd look around the room. You know, make sure no one's planted anything dangerous."

"Like what, Jordan?" Nick asked. "A bomb under our noses?"

"Or a bug or a hidden camera," Jordan shot back. "I would have thought one of you would have considered that."

"I didn't," Luke answered evenly. "Because there's no way anyone outside of our firm could have gotten access to Natalie's room." He shoved his gun back in its holster and Nick did the same. "You know protocol," he said. "Entering a client's private domain without explicit permission is prohibited. And I'm not sure I buy your reason. Let's go." He stepped back into the hallway and Jordan followed, looking completely unaffected.

"I was trying to be proactive," he said smoothly.

"Tell that to Roman, and the police," Luke said, grabbing his arm and escorting him down the stairs.

"What were you doing in my room?" Natalie's voice sounded from below, and she appeared at the foot of the stairs, Hunter at her side.

"Natalie, head on back to the security office," Luke said, but she stood her ground as if she hadn't heard him.

Jordan stopped and stared hard at Natalie when they reached the bottom of the stairs.

"You had something to do with it," he bit out, even as Luke and Nick forced him away from her and toward the front door. "He wouldn't have skipped town on his own!" Jordan's voice was rising as he attempted to wrench away from their grasp. "And then you go off to some island to enjoy yourself?" He sneered as Nick threw open the front door. "Yeah, I searched your room. You see the reward the police are offering right now? Ten grand for any information leading to Kyle."

"And you thought you'd find information in Natalie's room?" Hunter asked, his voice hard.

Jordan shrugged. "Her story isn't exactly believable. And police'll have a hard time serving a warrant *here*," he pointed out with derision. "Seemed a logical place to look."

"You sure took a big risk for a quick payout," Natalie said. "Especially considering that Kyle showed up at my apartment hours ago. Alive and well."

Jordan hid his surprise and said nothing, spearing her with a cold look of hatred. A challenge, almost. And if Luke weren't on the job, he would have knocked the look right off his face. Instead, he yanked him forward and out the front door of the house.

It took nearly an hour to file the police report and send Jordan packing. Luke couldn't get rid of the guy soon enough. It took a lot to rile Luke up, but greed and a disregard for others stirred up his temper. He left Hunter in the security office and headed to the front of the house, where Natalie was waiting in her father's office.

"Everything under control?" Judge Harper asked as Luke entered.

"Yes, sir," Luke responded. "A police report was filed, and Jordan's been escorted from the property."

"Good." The judge frowned. "And the man on my property?"

"Arrested for trespassing. He's a reporter. Tabloid. Paid Jordan a thousand dollars to help him get onto the property."

"So, the flashes..." Natalie started, realization dawning on her face.

"Camera."

"I'd like to know how Jordan sneaked him onto my property," the judge said, his usually mellow expression replaced with a shrewd sense of judgment. And rightly so. Judge Harper was one of Shield's biggest residential clients. Even after the cutbacks, he still invested a large sum into the security of his property.

"We're investigating," Luke said, the weight of the situation heavy on his shoulders. The Harper estate used his security system exclusively. "I'd offer an apology, but no amount of apologizing can erase what happened. The best I can promise you is that we'll get to the bottom of it, and give you a full report by noon tomorrow."

"Good," the judge said again, but he didn't look at all pleased. "Now, maybe you can help me with another problem."

"I'll do my best."

The judge slanted a disgruntled look at Natalie. "Seems my daughter's determined to move back into her apartment, get back to work, go about life as if some lunatic isn't stalking her."

"First of all, to be fair, tonight doesn't seem to be related to whoever's been stalking me," Natalie began.

She looked up at him, calm determination in her eyes. "Secondly, Roman's on board and I'm hiring a Shield team myself for my apartment until the guy's caught.

My place is easier to secure, anyway, and I've got to find some sort of normalcy."

"You've barely been back two days," her father pointed out.

"Dad, do you really think I'm safer here, or do you just not want me out of your sight?"

To Judge Harper's credit, he seemed to consider the question for a moment before answering. "If you're staying at your apartment, you're probably just as safe there," he agreed. "But if you're traveling to and from work, out and about in public…"

"How long am I supposed to hide?" she countered, frustration edging her voice.

Her father sighed, resigned. "Don't see why you can't stay here for a few weeks."

"I'll be here a couple more days, until everything's set up." She hugged him. "It's been a long day, Dad. We both need sleep. Things will look different in the morning."

"Try to get some sleep, okay?" Luke said.

She nodded. "I need to. Tomorrow will be a full day. I'm dropping my ring off with Hannah on my way to lunch with Julianna. Then I've got a work meeting."

Luke had been hoping she'd stick close to home base for a while.

"I can have someone drop the ring off," he suggested.

"It's on the way to the Montgomerys'," Natalie said. "And I haven't seen Hannah in weeks. I'd rather go myself."

Judge Harper looked like he was about to argue, but Luke caught his eye. "We'll take care of her," he said. He just hoped her father hadn't lost all his faith in their company after tonight's incident.

"I'll be ready to head out at around ten."

"Sounds good. I'll have the car out front." He excused

himself and left the house to check the property perimeter and run a test of the security system. He had a feeling he knew exactly how Jordan had sneaked the reporter in, and he was already devising solutions to prevent the same betrayal from ever happening again. Once he got that squared away, he'd need to talk to Roman about stepping away from Natalie's case. He frowned at the thought, but he knew it was the right thing to do.

Had his feelings for her clouded his judgment tonight? Would he have let any other client take a night run alone? Thankfully, the only surprise waiting for her on the garden trail had been a slimy reporter. But Luke was well aware of the fact that anyone could have been hiding in the shadows tonight—and he would have only had himself to blame.

THIRTEEN

The next morning, Natalie got ready for the day and headed downstairs to her dad's office. She tapped on the open door and walked in to where he sat at his little table, Bible in hand. Through the bay window, the sun peeked out behind the trees several acres beyond. Its glow was a dismal gray-yellow behind thickening clouds. It matched the heavy weight of her heart, and Natalie glanced away.

"I'm heading out. Love you, Dad," she said softly, kissing his cheek.

"Love you, too," he said. "Remember, don't go anywhere alone."

She'd heard the instruction dozens of times over the course of her life. It used to drive her crazy. Now, it just made her sad. In some ways, her father was the strongest person she knew, but he was also the most broken. Natalie didn't blame him for that. His only son had been abducted while on a field trip to the Baltimore Aquarium. It should have been a fun, benign experience for Liam and his kindergarten buddies. Instead, he'd died that day, and a little bit of Natalie's parents had died, too. Liam's death had forever shaped their family, and fear had become a constant shadow.

By the time Natalie was a teenager, she had become

tired of it. Tired of self-defense classes and Stranger Danger workshops. Tired of constant security and banned sleepovers. What had happened to her brother would never happen to her, and she'd resented her father for his delusion that he had any control over the bad things that could come her way.

When she'd gone off to college eagerly at seventeen, she had tried to refuse her dad's offer of security, including a high-end surveillance system in her dorm, and a couple of bodyguards to keep an eye on her.

Dad, she'd pleaded years ago. *You've done everything you can to prepare me for the world. You have to let go and let me have some independence and privacy.*

The tears had flooded his eyes so quickly Natalie hadn't had any warning. They'd seemed to take her dad by surprise, too, his shoulders heaving under the strain of decades of grief.

At that moment, she knew she would accept a whole fleet of bodyguards if it made her dad feel better.

To compromise, she'd agreed to never walk alone at night and to carry mace wherever she went. When she'd later moved into an apartment, she'd agreed to a security system. But she'd become complacent about security over the years.

Thankfully, her dad had known it. If he hadn't sent Luke after her to the Riviera, all his fears may have finally come true.

The thought unsettled her. Kyle may have returned, and she may have been in no real danger last night, but whoever had attacked her in Mexico, whoever had been waiting for her in her apartment in Charles Village, was still on the loose. She wouldn't feel safe again until he was caught, his motives revealed. She slipped on a pair of heeled sandals from the foyer closet and left the house, her heart already flipping at the sight of Luke waiting for her by the SUV.

"All set?" he asked, sunglasses shading his eyes as he opened the door for her.

She nodded, scooting across the seat and greeting Carson, who was driving.

"To Timeless Treasures, right?" Carson asked as Luke climbed in next to Natalie and shut the door.

"Right." She glanced over at Luke, her heart sinking at the rigid set of his shoulders, the sunglasses that hid his thoughts.

She refused to feel awkward. One incredible moment, one earth-shattering kiss, shouldn't ruin what felt like a growing friendship.

"You must be exhausted," she said finally, in an attempt at conversation.

"I'm used to it," he said simply.

"Did you figure out how the reporter got in?"

"Jordan turned off the motion detector to a far west section of the fence—for exactly forty-four seconds. At forty-five, an alarm would have sounded. Gave the reporter just enough time to get in."

"Wow. When did he do it?"

"Around 2:30 p.m. The guy pretty much set up a lookout behind one of the trees, obviously a spot Jordan had told him would avoid the cameras. He had a bunch of shots of you on his camera from earlier in the day. Guess he was camping out to get more."

"How do you keep that from happening again?"

"Simple. Some programming on the authorization system, and requirements for a supervisor override if anyone tries to turn off a sensor."

"Smart. Do you really think Jordan was looking for

evidence like he said he was? Something to link me to Kyle's disappearance?"

"Hard to say," Luke admitted. "What else could he have been looking for?"

"I don't know. Valuables? Money?"

"He's had other opportunities to look for those things, Natalie. He's been assigned security here before. And the reward the police were offering was enticing."

"But Shield pays well. He lost his job for a shot at ten grand."

"He wasn't banking on getting caught. The ten grand would have been a quick and easy bonus, especially if he kept his identity anonymous to the public."

"Will the police do anything about it?"

"I doubt there's much they *can* do about it," Luke said.

"It was breaking and entering, as far as I'm concerned," Natalie said.

"Police may or may not see it that way. Speaking of police, I had a message from Officer Canto earlier this morning. The guy trying to break into your room at the resort bribed a housekeeper. They caught and fired the housekeeper, but they didn't find the intruder."

"Probably because he followed me back here," she muttered.

"Maybe so. Looks like we're here." The SUV slowed in front of Timeless Treasures. The Masons had been in business for three generations and specialized in unique, high-quality craftsmanship. Hannah's dad, Ron, had always offered reasonable prices and done quality work, and Hannah was carrying on the family legacy. Natalie knew her friend would give an on-the-mark assessment of her ring.

Two small bells clanged gently against the glass door, signaling their entrance. Hannah looked up from a customer she was helping and excused herself. She wore a lilac blouse and black dress pants, her gorgeous red hair falling in pretty waves over her shoulders.

"Natalie!" Hannah cried, pulling her into a tight hug. Then her gaze moved to Luke.

"This is Luke," Natalie said. "He works for Shield."

Hannah smiled and shook his offered hand. "Nice to meet you."

Her attention switched back to Natalie, her smile falling. "I've been so worried... How *are* you?"

"That's a complicated question," she said, glancing around at the already busy shop.

"Maybe I can come by tonight?" Hannah suggested. "We can catch up?"

"That would be perfect."

She handed the ring to her friend.

Hannah held it delicately, her manicured nails a pretty pink.

"I've been secretly wanting to take a closer look at this since you got it."

"Why?" Luke asked.

Hannah laughed as if he had just told a very good joke.

"To see how close of a replica it is," she explained with an amused grin. "I'll take a look at it after lunch. I've got a couple of repairs to finish up first. Let me just log it in and give you a receipt."

Natalie laughed. "I trust you not to abscond with it."

"I'll be quick," Hannah said, and Natalie knew there'd be no arguing. Hannah was by the book, a rule follower to a T. "Hold on, though, I was just in the back looking for a new roll of printer paper." She set the ring in a midnight blue velvet tray and disappeared into the back.

"Unique place." Luke moved to a display of restored antique rings and pearl necklaces.

"The family's owned it for almost eighty years," Natalie said. "I've never visited a jewelry chain that even comes close."

"I've never seen rings like these," Luke agreed, turning the rotating display.

Natalie stepped closer to him, her arm brushing his. Several shimmering pearl necklaces hung in the display case, their gold clasps polished and shiny. "This necklace looks a lot like the one that was stolen."

"The family pearls?"

She nodded. "The only difference is the clasp. The one on my great-grandmother's necklace was really intricate. In fact, I brought it here for repair before the wedding because the clasp had broken."

"Wow. Your great-grandmother's? Quite an heirloom."

"Her husband gave it to her on their twenty-fifth wedding anniversary, and it's been passed to every Harper family bride ever since."

"Will you get a replacement?" he asked. "Start a new tradition?"

"I don't know," she said. "It won't be the same." Her heart sank at the realization, knowing that someone would wear that necklace and be oblivious to the generations of love it had wrapped around it. "It wasn't just the pearls. There was a tiny hand-stamped pendant at the back, hanging from the clasp. A heart."

"What was engraved on it?" He turned to her, his face so close she could see the gold specks in his deep brown eyes.

Something fluttered low in her belly. "Love never fails."

Natalie's words were whispered out soft and sure, like a promise, her nearness testing all the resolve Luke had managed to wrangle late last night and all through this morning. A touch of pink stained her cheeks, and she moved a step away, looking down at the diamond rings again. "I guess my great-grandmother was a romantic at heart. She and her husband were married for seventy-six years before he died. Her heart gave out the next day."

"Hence, the legacy behind the necklace," Luke re-marked. "I'm sorry it—"

"Okay, here we go," Hannah called as she came back into the room, a roll of printer paper in her hand. She quickly loaded the new paper and printed the receipt, yanking it from the dispenser and handing it to Natalie. "I think the media caught up with you. Sorry you've got to go face the dragons out there."

Natalie peeked out the front window and squared her shoulders. "Oh, that's nothing," she said with an easy smile. He could see her professionalism shine through, knew she was donning the public-relations cape. He ad-mired her for that as they said goodbye, and she walked outside with an unreadable face and relaxed posture.

There were at least seven reporters with cameramen and vans waiting outside, questions flying from every di-rection, and Natalie walked through the small crowd un-fazed, climbing into the SUV and settling in for the short ride as Carson pulled away from the little jewelry shop.

Luke glanced over at her, knowing it was time to tell her about the decision he'd made last night. "Hunter will meet us on-site to take over my shift," he said as the ve-hicle pulled onto the highway.

"Right. You've been working some serious overtime."

"It's not that, Natalie."

She met his gaze, a question in her eyes.

"I'm stepping away from your case."

A nearly imperceptible flash of hurt crossed her

face. The last thing he wanted to do was hurt her, and he rushed to explain.

"Last night, I knew better than to let you run alone. It was a decision that could have cost you your life." He didn't tell her that he'd realized he'd gotten too close to her, that his feelings for her had clouded his judgment.

"I insisted," Natalie pointed out quietly. "Plus, I wasn't actually in any danger. It was just a reporter."

"You could have been, though. That's the point. What if it hadn't been a reporter?"

"But—"

"I've already made the decision," he said, cutting her off. "It'll be better for both of us."

Natalie said nothing, but nodded and turned her attention out the window, and Luke couldn't help but wonder what might have been between them in another time and another place.

FOURTEEN

Natalie and Julianna had slipped off their shoes and gotten comfortable on cushioned porch rockers while Natalie described her bizarre encounter with Kyle and the incident back at her dad's house. In the back of her mind, though, she was reviewing the last conversation she'd had with Luke. It didn't make sense to be so crushed when she'd only known him for a handful of days. Maybe he was right about heightened emotions during trauma, but she didn't want to believe it. She'd let down her guard with Luke in a way she hadn't done with anyone else, had believed he had truly understood her—only to discover that he had no idea how deeply connected she felt with him.

Julianna sighed and set her barely touched plate of Thai food on the glass coffee table. "Kyle has something to do with all of this," she said with conviction, forcing Natalie's thoughts away from Luke. "The timing of his disappearance with everything you've been going through, and then he suddenly shows up at your door?"

The truth had begun to root itself in Natalie's gut, and she nodded. "I know. I just don't know how or why."

Julianna looked at her thoughtfully, her long black hair lying perfectly over her shoulders, her dark eyes sad and knowing. "Money is a motivator. If he was in as much trouble as it sounds like he was… Well, he knows your parents are pretty wealthy…"

It was back to the idea of kidnapping for ransom, which somewhat rang true, though she couldn't believe the man she had agreed to marry could stoop so low. "I don't know how he'd get the money to hire someone, though."

Julianna shrugged. "Maybe he made a deal. Offered a percentage of the ransom?"

Kyle's image flashed in Natalie's mind as she tried to imagine him even locating the resources to hire someone for such a job. It seemed too far-fetched, and a little humorous, to be honest. "This is real life, not a movie," she said with a small laugh.

Julianna smiled in return. "Maybe I've been in one too many thrillers." But her smile dropped a little when she added, "I never did like him, you know? And I can't believe he had the nerve to ask for the ring back."

"As strange as it sounds, I'm thinking of just giving it back."

"Oh?" Julianna asked the question with interest, not judgment, which was one of the reasons Natalie valued her friendship. She was an open person, always trying to understand other perspectives, never assuming her way was the right way.

"I don't want to keep it. And I don't need the money. My dad doesn't need the money."

Julianna nodded. "I doubt you'd get much for it, anyway," she pointed out. "If he never showed you the receipt, it's probably worth less than what he claimed he paid for it."

"I'll have my answer today. Hannah's looking at it, probably as we speak."

"Hannah?"

"My friend over at Timeless Treasures. She—"

"Oh, that's right," Julianna said, remembering. "I think I met her once."

"Probably at the New Year's gala. She took over the shop a few months ago. Her dad's pretty sick."

"Too bad about her dad. You know, I've never shopped there."

"You should go sometime. It's a unique little place and—"

Julianna stood up suddenly. "Sorry. I'll be right back."

"Sure." It was at least the fourth time Julianna had gone inside to *use the bathroom*. She was pregnant, so it made sense. Except that the last time, she'd been gone so long that Natalie had gone inside looking for her, only to find her on the phone. She'd been easily distracted during their lunch, and Natalie was trying not to let it bother her.

But when Julianna returned this time, she seemed more relaxed, and their conversation turned to the work meeting as the two sorted out a plan for what Natalie would tell her boss. The fund-raiser was a big deal. Julianna and other celebrities would be auctioning off famous jewelry they had worn in films and on red carpets, and it was guaranteed to bring in millions for pediatric mental health research. Julianna seemed to be waffling on her own contribution to the auction, kind of attached to the ring Natalie's engagement band had been fashioned after. But Natalie reminded her how important the cause was, and how they already had interested buyers willing to purchase the ring for more than double its value.

Eventually, her friend settled down, rubbing her tiny

belly and watching the quiet yard peacefully. Natalie sipped her water and glanced around. Montgomery property patrols passed by periodically, along with the two assigned Shield agents. Hunter, pulling a double shift, stood sentry on one side of the porch, while Nick, the agent who had helped Luke detain Jordan, patrolled the grounds.

A soft summer wind sifted through Natalie's hair, the scent of steamed rice and Asian spices mixing with the draft from the nearby garden, and for the first time in days, she felt somewhat relaxed and relatively safe, if not achingly disappointed.

She could almost relax. *Almost.* The copse of trees yards beyond still made her feel a little uneasy. Private property or not, security cameras or not, she knew that a determined person could find a way. She glanced over at Hunter. He was still standing, as he'd been for nearly an hour, refusing the offer of lunch or a seat, eyes trained on the world beyond the porch.

"You sure you don't want something to eat? There's plenty."

He turned his attention to her. "I ate before I came." He smiled warmly at her, his dimples making him appear younger than he probably was. She remembered his kids in the stroller, and wondered how old they were. Wondered what his story was.

The memory reminded her of Luke as he had leaned over his sister at the hospital, part brother, part parent. He was unlike anyone she'd ever met. And their kiss… Her heart raced as she let herself remember it. That kiss had been unlike any kiss she'd ever experienced.

Then he'd had to go and ruin it all. She frowned. But how could she be mad? She had vowed not to get involved with anyone for a year, and look what had happened in less than a week. Even in the best of circumstances, fast-moving relationships rarely led to forever. In a round-about sort of way, Luke was probably saving them both from a lot of heartache.

Except that her heart ached just thinking about him, remembering his small wave goodbye as Hunter came to take his place.

"We'll have to leave soon to make it to your meeting," Hunter pointed out, forcing her thoughts away from Luke.

"You're right. I'll—" Her cell rang next to her and she saw Hannah's number. "Hang on." She swiped to answer the call, curious to hear what her friend had discovered about the ring.

"Natalie."

The urgent tone of Hannah's voice made Natalie sit straight up. "What's wrong?" Her first thought was that Hannah's dad had taken a turn for the worse.

"Come straight here. Don't—" Hannah gasped, and Natalie stood, adrenaline making her shaky as she shoved her shoes back on and Hunter sent her a questioning look.

"Call 9-1-1," Hannah whispered, and the call ended.

"We have to get to Timeless Treasures," she told Hunter even as she punched in the emergency number. "That was Hannah. Something's happening at the shop."

Hunter opened the back door for her.

"What's going on?" Julianna asked, following them.

A dispatcher answered the phone, and Natalie waved Julianna off as she relayed what little information she had and hurried through the house with Hunter leading the way.

"I'll come with you!" Julianna offered, hastily pulling on a pair of shoes and grabbing her purse.

"I'm not authorized to take other passengers," Hunter said quickly.

"I'll meet you there!" Julianna shouted as Natalie and Hunter ran across the lawn to the waiting SUV, and Natalie prayed for the second time in as many days—this time that her friend would be okay.

"Bingo." Luke's pulse tripled when the home screen lit up on the phone in his hand. Roman was busy enjoying his first day as a father to the new baby, but not too busy to send Luke a contact who might be able to help him hack into Kyle's phone—the new Shield intern, Harrison Jenkins. He had arrived within a half hour, set up two computers, hooked up the phone, ran some code and smiled with satisfaction when his program worked.

Tall and lanky with a high-top fade, Harrison wore ripped jeans and bright white sneakers that matched his brilliant smile. Barely out of high school, he was a genius in the making. Luke hoped the kid had good influences in his life, because that kind of ability could easily be used for the wrong motives.

The teen scrolled through the phone as Luke watched, but it looked like the device had been cleared and reset.

"Nothing on it?" Luke asked, wondering why Kyle would have found his lost phone, reset it and then tucked it away in Natalie's office.

Harrison frowned, looking at the nearly full storage meter. "Oh, there's somethin' on it. Hang on."

With a little investigating, he found a hidden, password-protected app. And it didn't take him long to hack into it, either. What was inside was even more perplexing. Voice memos. Luke and Harrison exchanged a look and Harrison pressed Play on the first one. The voices were indistinguishable on the thirty-two-second clip, so he clicked on the second one.

Even by the fourth clip, he wasn't sure what—or who—he was listening to, but it sounded like a man and a woman in a romantic relationship.

"Well, I've gotta get out of here," Harrison said. "Unless you need something else?"

Luke thanked Harrison for his time and then pulled out a business card as an afterthought and handed it to the kid. "I'm in the process of starting up a nonprofit over in Cherry Hill. It'll be a community outreach for families, geared toward teens. If you're interested in mentoring some kids…"

Harrison's eyes lit up as he took the card and shoved it in his pocket. "Awesome."

"I'm planning to get some classes on the calendar for the fall and—"

Luke's cell rang and he glanced at it on the table next to him. Hunter. He'd only be calling if something was wrong.

"We're heading to Timeless Treasures," Hunter said when Luke picked up. "Police are on the way."

Luke was already grabbing his keys and waving Harrison out the door as Hunter filled him in on what little they knew. He ran to his room and loaded his weapon, then to Triss's room, tapping on the door before swinging it open.

She looked up from where she was sitting up in bed, her laptop open in front of her. Home from the hospital just hours ago, she was determined to get caught up with her summer class.

"There's trouble at the jewelry shop. I'm heading there."

"You have your vest?"

"In the car. Gotta go."

"Be careful!" she called after him, but he was already heading out the door. He barely took the time to lock up behind him, and told himself he'd put on the bulletproof vest when he arrived. The shop was less than eight minutes away—if he followed traffic laws.

He made it in just under six, throwing the car into Park and rushing up to the shop where several Shield agents had surrounded Timeless Treasures, Hunter at the door with breaching tools.

Luke charged across the sidewalk and up to Hunter's side just as the lock mechanism clicked.

"Got it," Hunter said, glancing back at Luke and waving for the rest of the team. "We're in."

As the team entered the shop, Luke realized too late he hadn't put on his vest. The silence inside only ratcheted up the tension. The front of the shop was empty, which brought them to the closed door leading to the back office. Luke reached out and twisted the knob. Unlocked. In one swift motion, he slammed the door wide open, and the team moved in like they'd been trained to do. Every glass case had been smashed, jewelry strewn around, computer equipment tossed. And there was blood. Blood on the tile floor and on the wall. From the thief reaching through smashed glass?

Then his attention caught on a lock of red hair and he holstered his weapon, rushing to the opposite side of the large workstation in the middle of the room. A smear of blood led to the tight space under the workstation that Hannah had fit herself into.

Luke crouched down, his heart in his throat as he took in the sight of her, curled up in the fetal position, her hair covering her face. "Hannah?" he said softly. "You're safe now. No one's going to hurt you."

When she didn't stir, he reached out and touched her hand. It was cool. Alarmed, he motioned to Hunter. "Help me get her out of here."

FIFTEEN

Hannah was limp but breathing, the side of her head bleeding profusely. From the sirens, it sounded like help was close.

Hunter shrugged out of his jacket, positioned himself on the floor behind her and pressed the wadded-up fabric to her wound. Her eyes flew open and she gasped, her gaze darting fearfully around the room.

She started to sit up, but Luke crouched over her, holding on to her arms, not sure about the extent of her injuries. "Easy," he said. "We're here to help you. An ambulance is on the way. Are you injured anywhere else aside from your head?"

"Where's Natalie?" she asked, her voice an urgent whisper.

"We'll get her in here," Hunter said, nodding to Nick.

"Tell us what happened," Luke said, trying to redirect her focus.

"I need to talk to Natalie." She'd started to tremble, likely the shock setting in. Luke radioed for Nick to bring a blanket with Natalie.

"She'll be here," he reassured her. "You're safe."

Seconds ticked by and Hannah stared up at him, but he wasn't sure she was really seeing him at all. Then her eyes closed again, her body limp.

Seconds later, Natalie rushed into the room, a blanket in her arms. She leaned over Natalie and tucked the blanket over her. "I'm here, Hannah," she said soothingly, but her fear was palpable. "I'm right here. The ambulance is pulling up now. You're going to be fine."

When Hannah didn't respond, Natalie looked up at Luke, tears welling in her eyes. The truth was, they didn't know if she would be fine. Thankfully, the paramedics had finally arrived. They burst into the shop, and Hannah was whisked away as police descended on the scene, dusting for prints, interviewing and taking photos.

Not for one minute did Luke believe the robbery had been random. Not when it was timed so closely with when Natalie dropped off her ring. He explained his theory to the police, but they were more interested in getting their hands on the shop's surveillance videos than entertaining his theories.

It was hours before the police finished photographing and cataloging the scene. By the time the Shield team was given the go-ahead to start cleaning up, it was well after ten, the night pitch-black.

Natalie had left hours ago to spend time at the hospital with Hannah, who was still heavily sedated, but recovering, after undergoing surgery to stop a brain bleed.

Luke had almost volunteered to accompany her, but Julianna had beat him to it, Carson and Nick on transport duty.

"We'll clean up the glass and blood," Hunter said next to him as police cars began to disperse. "Hannah's brother will be here soon."

Her brother, Landon, had taken the first flight he could get out of Atlanta when they'd finally been able to contact him. It seemed like the right thing to do to clean up the shop a little so he would have less to deal with when he arrived.

Luke began to walk with Hunter back toward the shop when headlights turned onto the dark street, Carson pulling up to the curb. Nick hopped out of the passenger seat and opened the back door, and Natalie climbed out, with Julianna following.

Luke's heart clenched at the sight of her. Her hair was limp, tucked behind her ears, a hint of mascara smudged under tired eyes. Every instinct told him to offer her a hug, but he forced himself to stand by his decision.

"How is she?" he asked.

"Still out," Natalie answered, "but the doctors are hopeful." She glanced toward the shop. "Are you done here?"

"Almost. Nick and I are going to clean up a bit before Hannah's brother gets here."

"I'll help," she offered.

"It's been a long day. You should get back home."

She was already marching up to the shop. "I'll never sleep. I'd like to help."

Julianna followed at her heels, and the two got to work alongside Luke and Hunter. Natalie's determination didn't surprise Luke, but Julianna's did.

She had an air of superficiality about her on-screen whenever he'd seen her in the news, but in real life, she adapted to the situation. She tied her hair into a quick bun, helped sweep up glass and inventory jewelry and spent a significant amount of time talking with and consoling Natalie.

Even with Nick patrolling outside the shop, they still had four sets of hands, so the clean-up was going quickly, and by the time Hannah's brother arrived, there was little left to be done. The repairs would have to wait until the Mason family could take care of them, but at least Landon hadn't arrived to the sight of broken glass and his sister's blood.

Landon was a young man of few words, nearly six-three with strawberry blonde hair a much lighter shade than his sister's. He'd thanked the crew for their help and almost immediately pulled his laptop out of his carry-on and logged into the shop's Wi-Fi.

His mission quickly became clear: he was logging into the security account. The police had confiscated the trashed computers, but there were other ways to access the footage from earlier in the day. "I'll be out front with Nick," Hunter said to Luke. "Radio when you're ready to head out." He left the room as the others in the room began to gather near Landon, anticipation thrumming as they waited for the surveillance video to appear on the screen.

Landon scrolled through the footage and started rolling it at 1:00 p.m., the screen showing Hannah in the back room, alone. She had taken Natalie's ring and was using tools to inspect it. Her facial expression was hidden, her head bent down, focusing on her work. But at a certain point she seemed to freeze, and Luke watched the video, adrenaline rushing. Was this the point where she heard the intruder? Video from the front of the store stood silent, though, not a customer around. Did she just sense something was wrong?

Suddenly, she was moving again, but her movements were hurried, almost panicky. She grabbed her pen and started scribbling something on a pad of paper, then tore the sheet out and folded it into a square. Grabbing the ring, she carefully placed it inside a small lined ring box, and then crossed the room to a center display where ring orders and repairs were stored. She flipped up a small panel in the center of the workstation and made a motion that resembled punching numbers on a safe. Luke couldn't see in great detail but sure enough, a small drawer rose up from the center of the workstation. Hannah placed the box and the paper in the drawer and then closed it again. Then she practically ran over to her cell phone on the opposite counter.

"She was in a real hurry," Natalie commented, her voice hushed.

"But not at first." Landon backed the footage up and they watched again, catching the moment when her methodical ring appraisal seemed to suddenly become an urgent mission.

It was difficult to watch the scene unfold after she'd secured the ring. Hannah had started to make a call when the front door opened and a man stepped inside, looking around the front room. He wore a business suit and a nylon mask, and he set a briefcase down just inside the door. In the back room, Hannah's posture stilled, the phone to her ear. She seemed to know instinctively something was wrong, but how could she? The man locked the door behind him, switched the sign to Closed and shut the blinds.

"That must have been when she called me," Natalie whispered, watching with horror.

The robbery lasted less than three minutes. Hannah's brother sat rigid and emotionless as they watched the man burst into the workroom, Hannah dropping her phone and running for the exit. But she didn't make it far. He leaped over the workstation and pounced on her slight frame, smashing her head into the ground and then into the corner edge of a cabinet.

"Oh, my gosh," Natalie said, and Julianna gasped, her hand covering her mouth. Luke's horror matched theirs as the man pushed up from where Hannah lay and ran back to the front of the shop for his briefcase. He pulled out a metal tool and began smashing glass with it, grabbing everything he could get his hands on quickly and stuffing the items into the briefcase.

He then ran to the back room, doing another quick smash-and-grab before making a hasty escape out the back of the shop.

Nearly a minute ticked by before Hannah started to move. It was painful to watch. She tried to stand, but seemed dazed and weak. Instead, she crawled, blood dripping from her head wound and down her shoulder, trailing alongside her on the floor. She reached up and locked the back door, then grabbed her phone and crawled to the place where they had found her nearly unconscious, but she seemed to pass out then, the phone falling from her hands. Minutes passed slowly and the shop stood still until the Shield team entered.

"That's horrible!" Julianna said, clearly shaken. "He nearly killed her."

Luke crossed the room to the broken display case, scanning the intact gray granite workspace in the center for the panel that Hannah had accessed.

Natalie appeared at his side, running her hand along the surface.

"Here," Landon said, maneuvering around the group. He depressed a nearly invisible button in the granite countertop, which released a panel opening to a keypad. He punched in a code, and the drawer elevated out from the workstation.

Natalie reached in and pulled out the box with the ring, opening it as Luke pulled out the paper and unfolded it. Julianna and Landon hovered between them as they all looked at the appraisal together.

Luke skimmed the handwritten form and instinctively backed up, trying to make sense of what he was seeing.

"What?" Natalie was the first to speak, looking up from the form to Julianna and then Luke.

Hannah had appraised the ring at $1.4 million. She had noted every technical detail of the stones, and then she had written a note in the comments section that the ring appeared to be not a replica, but the original ring owned by Julianna Montgomery.

Julianna's olive skin looked suddenly pale, and she held out her hand, showing them her own ring. "Impossible."

But she looked uneasy, more than surprised.

"This doesn't make any sense," Natalie said, opening the ring box to take another look. "How would I have your ring?"

Luke's mind circled back to the recordings on Kyle's phone. Clearly a conversation between lovers. Had it been Julianna's voice he'd heard?

"Let's compare." Julianna pulled off her ring and held it in her palm, holding her other hand out for the newly appraised ring.

Natalie started to hand the ring over, but Luke intercepted it, setting it back in the locked compartment for the time being, keeping his eyes on Julianna the whole time.

Her eyes seemed a little wild, unfocused. He had no idea what was going on, but he knew he needed to call the police back to the scene, and also turn over Kyle's cell phone. "This is probably a matter for the police," he said, pulling out his phone.

"Don't do that." Julianna's voice was soft and pleading, her eyes suddenly filling with tears. "It's my ring. I can—I can explain."

He ignored her pleas as the phone rang and he spoke with the detective about the appraisal and the cell phone recordings. As he spoke, Julianna started to back away, one slow step at a time.

Then she reached into her purse.

The gun was in her hand before Luke could even register what was happening. She held it shakily, not aimed anywhere in particular.

"Get down!" Luke yelled to Natalie and Landon, but he didn't have time to see if they'd followed instructions. He lunged toward Julianna, yelling for backup as she raised the weapon.

"Don't come any closer," she said, her voice shaky, tears streaming down her face. And she put the gun to her own temple.

"No! Julianna! Don't!" Natalie screamed, suddenly rushing forward, but Luke maneuvered in front of her.

"Stay back."

Slowly, he approached Julianna. "You don't want to do this," he said gently. "Think about your baby." But her eyes were glazed over, and he wasn't sure she was even hearing a word he was saying.

Behind her, Hunter and Nick had appeared in the doorway, and he made eye contact. Together, they would try to get the gun away from her before she could pull the trigger. When Luke stepped forward, they would act. It was an unspoken agreement.

Luke rushed Julianna as Hunter and Nick simultaneously dragged her down, an anguished scream ripping from her throat as she fell. But as Luke grabbed her gun arm to disarm her, she jerked wildly away and a loud blast filled the small shop.

Luke flew backward, sprawled out on the freshly mopped tile, every muscle suddenly heavy, time slowing down.

His vision blurred as Natalie's face suddenly appeared

over him. Tears streaming down her red cheeks, her voice sounded far away as she shouted for something or someone. Then she was pressing something to his chest, her face inches from his.

"Don't cry," he whispered, and somehow his hand came up to brush tears from her cheek.

"I'm not crying," she said, more tears falling.

This wasn't the way he wanted to die; those weren't the last words he wanted to exchange. But his hand dropped, and his eyes closed, and the last words he heard were Natalie whispering, "Don't die, don't die, don't die."

Luke opened his eyes to darkness and the low whir of machines. He tried to sit up, but his muscles wouldn't cooperate. He felt nothing. No pain, no nausea. He knew he was in the hospital, and in a flash everything came back to him. Fear struck all at once. He couldn't feel anything. Had the shot paralyzed him? Gone through his chest to his spine? He wiggled his fingers, his hands. No, not paralyzed. But he couldn't seem to move his larger muscle groups. He shifted his right arm to try to get leverage to scoot up in the bed, and realized he wasn't alone.

His vision cleared as he looked down at Natalie's near-white hair on the bed next to him. She'd pulled a chair up close, curled up and laid her head next to him. New emotions welled up as he remembered her tears and her pleading with him not to die. He set his hand down on her head, gently stroking the tangled waves as she slept.

The bullet could have just as easily found her, and the thought turned his stomach. He had a feeling Julianna hadn't meant to shoot. Could see her face in his memory as he fell. She'd dropped the gun, screaming, but it had been too late.

Natalie stirred and sat up suddenly, her gaze finding

his in the dark. "You're awake," she said, reaching for the nurse call button, but he set his hand on her arm.

"I'm okay. How long have we been here?"

She looked at her phone. "It's almost seven in the morning. You were in surgery until three. Do you remember coming out of it?"

He shook his head.

"They said you'd sleep a lot. Are you in pain?"

"No."

The room seemed lighter now that his eyes had adjusted to the dark, the glow of the machines playing on Natalie's face. She had never looked more beautiful, even with mascara smudged, hair in disarray, T-shirt sleep-rumpled.

"Tell me what happened."

"It *was* Julianna's ring. She and Kyle had an affair. He was sneaky enough to record some of their interactions. Stole the ring from her one night after she'd been drinking, swapped it with the replica he'd originally bought for me. Then used the ring and the recordings as a bribe."

"For money."

She nodded. "He wanted a hundred grand and he'd destroy the recordings and return the ring. But she couldn't get ahold of a hundred grand without her husband finding out. She fed him a couple thousand at a time. Hired some help to get the ring back. That's what happened the morning of the wedding. The guys she hired showed up and knocked him around, tore up his apartment looking for the recordings and threatened to kill him if the ring wasn't back by midnight."

Luke thought about that for a minute. "So he got scared and skipped town."

The look of disgust on Natalie's face was all the answer he needed.

"Then the guys came after you."

She nodded. "She didn't want to kill me, isn't that nice?" she asked sarcastically. "She just wanted to get rid of the evidence of the affair and make sure no one caught wind of the fact that I had her ring. That would be hard for anyone to explain."

"Wow." He had suspected all along Kyle had something to do with the attacks, but he never would have imagined a story like this one. "Wonder how he planned to swap the ring out later."

Natalie shrugged. "I had told him it needed to be resized. My guess is he'd planned to find a way to swap it back then."

Luke shook his head. "Too bad Julianna couldn't have just come clean. She dug herself a much deeper hole."

Natalie frowned, sadness passing through her eyes. "I don't really know. I would guess that after spending years making a life for herself as a successful actress and a name for herself as a champion for mental health, she couldn't bear the thought of losing it all. Plus, she announced publicly before Christmas that she'd be auctioning off her ring at the fund-raiser in July. She'd look like a fraud once the buyer took it to an appraiser."

"What a shame," Luke said, and he really did mean it. Julianna had had the world at her feet, and she had thrown it away.

"It really is. Especially because I don't really think she was in her right mind. But she'll still do jail time. So will Kyle—for extortion, bribery and obstruction of justice."

"So Jordan really wasn't involved?"

"Doesn't look like he did anything but snoop in my room and exercise poor judgment. The reporter checked out."

"Help me sit up a little?"

She pressed the adjustment arrow on the bed control

panel, and he set his hand on the bed to push up a little, but it connected with something hard. A book? He looked down and saw what Natalie had fallen asleep on.

"Where'd the Bible come from?" he asked, surprised.

"I asked my dad to bring it."

"What were you reading?"

"He suggested *Psalms*." She smiled softly. "To be honest, I couldn't tell you what I read. But there was something peaceful about reading it out loud."

Then her expression changed, a wave of indecision passing through her eyes. The moment stretched silent and full of thoughts unspoken.

"What is it?" Luke asked finally, his eyes searching hers.

She hesitated a fraction of a second and then leaned in close, her hand settling on his cheek. His pulse quickened at her touch. "I have never prayed so hard in my life," she said, her voice a near-whisper. "You almost died, Luke. She almost killed you." Her eyes teared up, but then she grinned. "And I would have never gotten the chance to tell you how wrong you were."

He laughed softly, surprised at her words. "Well, thank goodness for that."

She looked straight into his eyes, fingers sweetly stroking the side of his face. "This…whatever this is between us…it's not an illusion. From the moment we met, every time we've been apart, I've missed you." He read uncertainty in her eyes, knew the vulnerability she battled.

He also knew in that heartbeat that what he'd thought about them had been all wrong. His connection with Natalie was special, forged through the intertwining of hearts and souls—not simply shared trauma.

He reached up and took her hand, gently moving it from

his face to just over his heart, his other hand joining in on what felt like a promise.

"I have never been so wrong in my life," he agreed.

Natalie smiled and laid her head on his shoulder, her hair tickling his chin. He turned toward her and kissed the top of her head, daring to hope for what he'd almost given up on: a future with this woman who made him smile, helped him dream and stood by him in the darkest moments.

EPILOGUE

Three Months Later...

Natalie stepped off the ladder, bare feet crinkling the plastic drop cloth. She reached to fold the ladder, but Luke turned the corner and took over. He folded it up and leaned it against a far wall, then slid his arms around her from behind and pressed a kiss near her ear. "You did a great job."

She eyed the verse stenciled along the wall in metallic midnight blue. *Now faith is the substance of things hoped for, the evidence of things not seen.* Hebrews *11:1.* She'd placed it in the entryway of the Cherry Hill Community Center, so it was the first thing people would see as they walked in.

"It made me think of all these kids. Of new hope." She turned in his arms, slid her hands over his shoulders.

"It's perfect," he responded, and he cast a glance around the room. His eyes reflected the reality of the dream he'd been given all those years ago. He'd been bold enough to believe that something that sounded impossible would come to fruition—and it had.

"Just a few more minutes," Natalie said, and he looked back at her, his eyes bright with anticipation.

"Have you peeked outside?" he asked.

"No. This verse took me ages."

"Lots of news coverage," he said.

"And kids?"

He smiled. "More than I thought there'd be on open-ing day."

The entire building smelled like grilling burgers. Chances were the kids could smell the food from a mile away. Tonight was a community open house. A chance for kids and families alike to tour the facility.

And what a facility it was.

As restitution, Julianna's husband, Kenneth, had gifted the ring back to Natalie. Natalie would never wear it again, and she couldn't begin to consider using the money she'd get for it on herself, so she'd auctioned it off and given a significant portion of the proceeds to the Cherry Hill Community Center. The rest she'd used to create a schol-arship fund for youth members of Luke's community cen-ter.

"It's going to be great," she said.

"Let me go put this ladder away," Luke said. "Hang tight for a minute, okay? I have something for you."

With that, he moved away from the entry and left Nat-alie alone in the large room.

To her right was the game room, complete with a pool table, air hockey, pinball and foosball. To her left was the entrance to the cafeteria-style dining hall, where kids would be able to show up in the morning for a free break-fast, and in the afternoon for a snack or a hot meal.

Natalie had walked every square inch of the build-ing, awed by Luke's creativity and foresight. One wing held classrooms for community meetings and offices for free counseling. With the money from Julianna's ring, he'd been able to hire on two full-time counselors. He'd installed a library with plenty of tables for tutoring sessions, and a gym where Natalie would teach self-defense classes to kids, teens and women in the community. She'd picked up her own training again and was working toward her black belt.

It almost seemed too good to be true.

Luke appeared in the entryway, motioning for her to follow him. "Come on," he said, and her heart skipped a beat. She was pretty sure she knew where they were heading.

The only place she hadn't seen yet—and only because Luke insisted she wait until it was complete—was the chapel. Curiosity was killing her, but she'd managed to stay away from the northeast wing, where Luke had been quietly overseeing the only part of the community center that he'd refused her help with.

He grinned as she sidled up next to him, and he wrapped a hand around hers. They'd kept their relationship quiet and taken things slowly after she'd confided in him her one-year-without-a-man vow, which they'd both shared a laugh over. But in the past few months, they'd fallen into a rhythm of friendship and mutual trust and admiration she hadn't dreamed possible. She'd helped him get the community center in shape, painting, moving in furniture, staying up most of last night before the grand opening. Organizing the pantry and meal schedules. The time she spent there energized her almost as much as the time she and Luke spent together.

They walked at a clipped pace down the sunlit corridor, and Natalie glanced up at Luke. "Is it finally my turn to see the chapel?"

Double doors lay straight ahead and he nodded, pulling a door open for her. "After you."

Natalie stepped inside and froze. The floor was hardwood, the walls were painted a serene dove-gray and a backlit cross hung at the center of the wall beyond the stage. The donated pews would hold at least two hundred. She'd spotted Luke and Roman refinishing some of them in the courtyard earlier last week, and they gleamed now, upholstered in royal blue cushioning.

It was simple and beautiful.

And awash in candlelight.

Natalie cocked her head to the side in question. "Is someone getting married?"

For a breath, Luke didn't answer, but then his smile tugged up on one side. "Not tonight," he said, and walked down the aisle toward the pulpit.

Natalie followed, stepping up onto the stage with him and taking in the pews gleaming under dancing candle-light.

Then Luke reached into the pocket of his khakis.

He pulled out a slender rectangular box and handed it to Natalie.

Heart pounding, she tugged the lid off and pulled back a tiny bit of silver tissue paper hiding the gift inside.

Pearls winked up at her, and she drew in a sharp breath, her eyes flooding.

She stared down at the family necklace, at the hand-stamped pendant on its clasp, newly shined with the message generations of Harper women had passed along to the next.

Love never fails.

"You found it," she said, her throat tight with emotion.

Luke had called nineteen pawnshops and visited eleven before he found it. He would have searched a thousand more shops to be rewarded with the look in Natalie's eyes at that very moment.

He reached into the box and lifted out the necklace,

unclasping it. Moving behind Natalie, he settled the strand around her neck, his fingers grazing soft skin at her nape as he secured the fastener. She turned toward him, eyes shimmering, the pearls skimming her collarbone in stark contrast to the plain pink cotton tank top she'd paired with paint-splattered jean shorts.

"I figured you'd be needing it again someday," he said. "Soon," he added, and he caught the sweet curve of her mouth in a kiss.

She pulled back a fraction of an inch, and for one alarming moment, he wondered if he'd said too much, too fast.

But she looked him straight in the eye, and the candlelight danced there, brilliant and full of life. "I guess this means I'll have to break my promise."

He laughed softly. "I'll wait nine more months, if you want to finish out your year of singlehood."

It was Natalie's turn to laugh. "I never would have made that promise if I'd known you...if I'd known what I'd been missing."

"Well, then, I say you're off the hook."

Natalie grinned. "I love you," she whispered.

"You stole my next line," he said, tugging her closer.

She pressed her lips together in a smile she couldn't contain.

"Don't let me stop you."

"I love you, too," he said, his mouth inches from hers.

She leaned up and met him there, her lips soft on his, her hand curving along the back of his neck.

A baby cooed.

A baby?

Luke pulled away and swiveled to the chapel entrance. "I knew it!" Kristin stood just inside the doorway, the bean (since named Ivy) tucked securely into a floral-print sling over her chest.

Luke felt himself grinning at her sparkling smile. He and Natalie had been careful to keep their romance private in the wake of all the publicity, but it was time to move on from the past and let the chips fall wherever they would.

"People are getting antsy out there," Kristin said. "You coming? Or should I invite them all in here for an impromptu wedding ceremony?"

"Kristin!" Natalie chastised, laughing.

Her sister shrugged good-naturedly. "I'm just calling it like I see it. A church. Candlelight. The family wedding necklace. And a kiss that just put a blush on a mother of four. So, what's it gonna be?"

"We're coming," Natalie said, stepping down off the stage.

Luke walked with her and caught sight of Kristin's baby peeking over the edge of the sling. She had a little tuft of white hair in the middle of her head and blue curious eyes. Those eyes kindled memories of his sister, his clumsy attempts at comforting her in the middle of the night, the way she'd curl into his chest and suck on anything he could offer her—from a pacifier he'd rescued from a mall playground to her chubby little thumb whenever the pacifier had gone missing.

For the first time in years, he thought he could do that again. And better this time. After all, he'd had plenty of practice. And this time, he wouldn't be doing it alone.

He grabbed hold of Natalie's hand as he pushed the door open to bright sunlight, a mass of smiling faces and reporters at the ready.

Kristin moved into the crowd, taking a place by her husband and their kids, flanked by William and Stacy

Harper. Ella held baby Lillie in a sling next to Roman, whose dark glasses hid his expression, but Luke caught his nod of encouragement. Several Shield employees had come to support the endeavor, too, including Harrison Jenkins, who would be heading up a computer science club at the center starting next month. Luke's sister had found a spot close to the front of the crowd, beaming a rare smile Luke had waited years to see again.

Natalie held out a giant pair of scissors someone passed her, gesturing to the red ribbon separating the crowd from the entrance. She smiled up at him, her eyes dancing in the late-September sunshine. "You ready?" she asked.

He wrapped his hand around hers on the scissors and they maneuvered the tool together toward the ribbon. "More than you know," he said, and as the scissors sliced through ribbon, he kissed her. Cheers and whistles and camera flashes erupted around them, and Natalie smiled against his lips, pulling back just a little.

"Our secret's out, then," she whispered, her eyes shimmering with humor.

He glanced out at their audience, catching the smiles on faces of friends and family. No one looked the least bit surprised.

"I'm not sure we've ever managed to fool anyone but ourselves," he responded as the doors behind them opened to his dream that had finally come to pass. Only it was better than he'd ever envisioned. He tugged Natalie to his side so they could let the crowd file in ahead of them. All those years he'd imagined this day, but he'd never imagined he'd have someone to share it with.

Natalie leaned her head against his shoulder as a cool autumn wind blew her hair into his face. He smoothed it down and pressed a kiss to the top of her head.

"I sure hope you're in this for the long haul," he whispered into her ear.

Natalie lifted her face to meet his gaze, her hand coming up to the pearls at her neck. The necklace had shifted, the pendant shimmering under the sun.

Love never fails.

"I can't imagine doing life with anyone else," she said.

"Let's get started, then," he responded, and led her through the threshold, his heart brimming over with a sense of completeness he'd longed for all his life.

* * * * *

If you liked this story from Sara K. Parker,
check out her previous books:

Undercurrent
Dying To Remember

Available now from Love Inspired Suspense!

Find more great reads at
www.LoveInspired.com

Dear Reader,

Trauma leaves an imprint on the soul. We are told in the Book of John that we'll face trouble as we pass through this life, but that knowledge doesn't protect us from the pain. Some days, it simply hurts to take each breath. Some weeks, we lose the ability to smile and truly laugh. Some painful seasons, it's almost impossible to believe that God is near. Natalie and Luke both faced seasons of despair in their lives, but opened their hearts to the way God was working to make all things new. While the blessings that come in the wake of trauma will never erase the grief of a heart torn to shreds, each new sunrise is a reminder that we're not alone—every blessing a promise that the Lord still has good in store.

Love,
Sara K. Parker

P.S. I love to hear from readers—find me at www. sarakparker.com.

JUSTICE MISSION
True Blue K-9 Unit • by Lynette Eason
After K-9 unit administrative assistant Sophie Walters spots a suspicious stranger lurking at the K-9 graduation, the man kidnaps her. But she escapes with help from Officer Luke Hathaway. Now, with her boss missing and threats on Sophie's life escalating, can Luke and his K-9 partner save her?

RESCUING HIS SECRET CHILD
True North Heroes • by Maggie K. Black
Trapped with armed hijackers aboard a speeding train in the northern Ontario wilderness, army corporal Nick Henry is determined to free the innocent hostages—especially when he realizes that includes his high school sweetheart, Erica Knight, and the secret son he never knew he had.

IDENTITY: CLASSIFIED
by Liz Shoaf
Someone is convinced security specialist Chloe Spencer has a disc that belongs to him, and he's willing to kill to get it back. But with Sheriff Ethan Hoyt at her side, can she uncover the truth about her past and take down the killer before it's too late?

LETHAL RANSOM
by Laurie Alice Eakes
When Kristen Lang's federal judge mother is kidnapped, the culprits have one ransom demand—her life for her mother's. But Deputy US Marshal Nick Sandoval refuses to let her make the trade. Can he succeed in his mission to keep both Kristen and her mother alive?

UNDERCOVER JEOPARDY
by Kathleen Tailer
Taken hostage in a bank robbery, the last person Detective Daniel Morley expects to find disguised as a robber is his ex-fiancée, FBI agent Bethany Walker. Now, with a mole in law enforcement putting Bethany's life in danger, the only way Daniel can protect her is by joining her undercover.

REUNION ON THE RUN
by Amity Steffen
Framed for her husband's murder and on the run from both the killer and the police, Claire Mitchell needs help if she wants to survive. But when it arrives in the form of her ex-boyfriend, former army ranger Alex Vasquez, can she trust him with her life...and her heart?

Get 4 FREE REWARDS!

We'll send you 2 FREE Books plus 2 FREE Mystery Gifts.

Love Inspired® Suspense books feature Christian characters facing challenges to their faith... and lives.

FREE
Value Over
$20

YES! Please send me 2 FREE Love Inspired® Suspense novels and my 2 FREE mystery gifts (gifts are worth about $10 retail). After receiving them, if I don't wish to receive any more books, I can return the shipping statement marked "cancel." If I don't cancel, I will receive 4 brand-new novels every month and be billed just $5.24 each for the regular-print edition or $5.74 each for the larger-print edition in the U.S., or $5.74 each for the regular-print edition or $6.24 each for the larger-print edition in Canada. That's a savings of at least 13% off the cover price. It's quite a bargain! Shipping and handling is just 50¢ per book in the U.S. and 75¢ per book in Canada.* I understand that accepting the 2 free books and gifts places me under no obligation to buy anything. I can always return a shipment and cancel at any time. The free books and gifts are mine to keep no matter what I decide.

Choose one: ☐ **Love Inspired® Suspense Regular-Print** (153/353 IDN GMY5) ☐ **Love Inspired® Suspense Larger-Print** (107/307 IDN GMY5)

Name (please print)

Address   Apt. #

City   State/Province   Zip/Postal Code

Mail to the Reader Service:
IN U.S.A.: P.O. Box 1341, Buffalo, NY 14240-8531
IN CANADA: P.O. Box 603, Fort Erie, Ontario L2A 5X3

Want to try 2 free books from another series? Call 1-800-873-8635 or visit www.ReaderService.com.

SPECIAL EXCERPT FROM

When K-9 administrative assistant Sophie Jordan sees someone tampering with her boss's notes, she finds herself in a killer's crosshairs. Can NYPD K-9 cop Luke Hathaway and his partner keep her safe?

Read on for a sneak preview of
Justice Mission *by Lynette Eason,*
the thrilling start to the True Blue K-9 Unit series,
available in April 2019 from Love Inspired Suspense!

Get away from him.

Goose bumps pebbled Sophie Jordan's arms, and she turned to run. The intruder's left hand shot out and closed around her right biceps as his right hand came up, fingers wrapped around the grip of a gun. Sophie screamed when he placed the barrel of the weapon against her head. "Shut up," he hissed. "Cooperate, and I might let you live."

A gun. He had a gun pointed at her temple.

His grip tightened. "Go."

Go? "Where?"

"Out the side door and to the parking lot. Now."

"Why don't you go, and I'll forget this ever happened?"

"Too late for that. You're coming with me. Now move!"

"You're *kidnapping* me?" She squeezed the words out, trying to breathe through her terror.

Still keeping his fingers tight around her upper arm, he gave her a hard shove and Sophie stumbled, his grip the only thing that kept her from landing on her face.

Her captor aimed her toward the door, and she had no choice but to go. Heart thundering in her chest, her gaze jerked around the empty room. No help there. Maybe someone would be in the parking lot?

Normally, her penchant for being early averted a lot of things that could go wrong and usurp her daily schedule. Today, it had placed her in the hands of a dangerous man— and an empty parking lot in Jackson Heights. Where was everyone?

Think, Sophie, think!

A K-9 SUV turned in and she caught a glimpse of the driver. Officer Luke Hathaway sat behind the wheel of the SUV. "Luke!"

With a burst of strength, she jabbed back with her left elbow. A yell burst from her captor along with a string of curses. She slipped from his grip for a brief second until he slammed his weapon against the side of her head.

Don't miss
Justice Mission *by Lynette Eason,*
available April 2019 wherever
Love Inspired® Suspense books and ebooks are sold.

www.LoveInspired.com

LISEXP0319

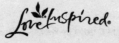

They'd both just turned back to their work when a familiar loud, croaking sound cut the silence.

The twins shrieked and ran from where they'd been playing into the little cabin's yard and slammed into Anna, their faces frightened.

"What was that?" Anna sounded alarmed, too, kneeling to hold and comfort both girls.

"Nothing to be afraid of," Sean said, trying to hold back laughter. "It's just egrets. Type of water bird." He located the source of the sound, then went over to the trio, knelt beside them, and pointed through the trees and growth.

When the girls saw the stately white birds, they gasped.

"They're so pretty!" Anna said.

"Pretty?" Sean chuckled. "Nobody from around here would get excited about an egret, nor think it's especially pretty." But as he watched another one land beside the first, white wings spread wide as it skidded into the shallow water, he realized that there was beauty there. He just hadn't noticed it before.

That was what kids did for you: made you see the world through their fresh, innocent eyes. A fist of longing clutched inside his chest.

The twins were tugging at Anna's shirt now, trying to get her to take them over toward the birds. "You may go look as long as you can see me," she said, "but take careful steps by the water." She took the bolder twin's face in her hands. "The water's not deep, but I still don't want you to wade in. Do you understand?"

Both little girls nodded vigorously.

They ran off and she watched for a few seconds, then turned back to her work with a barely audible sigh.

"Go take a look with them," he urged her. "It's not every day kids see an egret for the first time."

"You're sure?"

"Go on." He watched her run like a kid over to her girls. And then he couldn't resist walking a few steps closer and watching them, shielded by the trees and brush.

The twins were so excited that they weren't remembering to be quiet. "It caught a *fish*!" the one was crowing, pointing at the bird, which, indeed, held a squirming fish in its mouth.

"That one's neck is like an S!" The quieter twin squatted down, rapt.

Anna eased down onto the sandy beach, obviously unworried about her or the girls getting wet or dirty, laughing and talking to them and sharing their excitement.

The sight of it gave him a melancholy twinge. His own mom had been a nature lover. She'd taken him and his brothers fishing, visited a nature reserve a few times, back in Alabama where they'd lived before coming here.

Oh, if things were different, he'd run with this, see where it led…

Don't miss
Lee Tobin McClain's Low Country Hero,
available March 2019 from HQN Books!

www.Harlequin.com

PHLTMEXP0319